JESSICA TREAT

A Robber in the House

for Graciela:
Hope you enjoy these
small stories —
con cariño
dic. 2005

COFFEE HOUSE PRESS :: MINNEAPOLIS :: 1993

Acknowledgment is made to the following publications in which some of these stories first appeared: *Alaska Quarterly Review, Asylum, Bottomfish, Brooklyn Review, Dog River Review, Mudfish, The Paper Bag, Paragraph, The Prose Poem.* "Home" was anthologized in *Word of Mouth, Volume 2* (Crossing Press).

With thanks to Rilla, Jonathan, and Henrik whose insight helped to shape this book.

Coffee House Press books are available to the trade through our primary distributor, Consortium Book Sales & Distribution, 1045 Westgate Drive, Saint Paul, MN 55114. For personal orders, catalogs or other information, write to us at 27 North Fourth Street, Suite 400 Minneapolis, MN 55401

Library of Congress CIP Data
Treat, Jessica, 1958-
    A Robber in the House/Jessica Treat.
    ISBN 1-56689-007-1 : $10.95
    I. Title.
    PS3570.R359R6   1993
    813'.54—dc20   93-17101, CIP

9 8 7 6 5 4 3 2

Contents

A ROBBER IN THE HOUSE

for
Henrik
and for that city of cities
(que me dió tanto)
México, D.F.

CAFE

A Part of Her

SHE WAS the kind of person who would find a small piece of glass in her sausage, take it out, and then keep on eating. Once we were having breakfast in a restaurant and her potatoes arrived with a fly on them. A dead one. She didn't think I saw it, I could tell. I pretended not to notice as she carefully flicked it to one side, then dropped it to the floor very quietly. I watched her eat her potatoes. I couldn't help thinking about it. I thought it disturbed her too, I saw her wince; she was having trouble finishing them. "Why don't you send them back? How can you go on eating them?"

"What?" she said. She really seemed at first not to know what I was referring to. "Oh well," she said. "It was just a fly. People are so squeamish." She smiled then.

It was her smile that did it, the way it seemed to come from some hidden reservoir, a light source almost—no, I'm not explaining this well. It's that she wasn't beautiful; she was almost plain-looking, but when she smiled, it changed everything. It was a gift. She smiled and you felt warmed; you lost yourself a moment just looking at her. She caught you up in it and you suddenly wanted to be a part of her. It wasn't always like that. These were moments.

There's a War On

HE HAD a face like a teddy bear, not handsome at all, more like the teddy bear you'd forgotten, left in the corner because you found something better until one day you notice him: forgotten, forlorn, and suddenly guilt fills you and for a moment you can't decide whether to turn away or to hold him close to you.

He was very kind to her. He opened the door as she came in, closed it gently behind her. He was a gentleman, she could see that now. For so long she'd thought him crude, unshaven, but now she saw that she'd been mistaken.

At night when she walked by the café, looking but not venturing to go in, she'd suddenly see him staring out at her. And quickly she'd turn, hurry away from him. He seemed to be there whenever she was. He lived there as she did. But it bothered her that he should know no other life awaited her.

It scared her; he had that power. It seemed to her only a matter of time before she'd have to give in to him. Only a matter of time: his leg shook, his face twitched; he was waiting. She dared not look at him, meet his eyes, betray to him that she knew he knew. And what would happen then? Once, she'd dropped her spoon; it clattered to the floor and swiftly he'd picked it up for her (though he must know she wouldn't use it now?) and held it out to her. He'd smiled at her over his offering and she'd stared at it, before taking it, thanking him.

But for what? For providing for her surrender? Yet he seemed to know she wasn't ready; he still hadn't spoken to her. He still sat, nervously waiting. There was time yet.

She sat in her own corner, darker than his, not lit by the glass door. She felt his smile, his sad brown eyes, lock her in there. The waiters circled between them. She hadn't wanted them to know. She had feigned another life: she left the café always at five; she imagined a family for herself, work she must attend to; she'd seen that they imagined it as well. Now she felt cornered. The waiter already knew what she'd ask for. He brought it to her minutes after she sat down. Even the owner, who oversaw everything from his cappuccino machine, drawing the levers down then up with a certain urgency, seemed to be watching, waiting.

She saw it was all laid out: she was only a piece in a board game, part of a plan. He was the other piece, waiting in his corner, his square. He smiled at her sheepishly. She glared. He lowered his head to his coffee. She lifted hers. His leg shook; she held hers firmly. The air was thick, smelling of coffee and smoke, expectation fermenting.

But then a group of girls entered, some men, and voices of a higher pitch filled the room. She saw that darkness was outside, not in, and she could leave the café.

One day she arrived to find his move had been made. He sat in her corner, not his. She scanned the room. What did it mean? She sat down at the first table she found. But she felt confused. She looked at the waiter expectantly. He brought her her coffee. Her hand shook as she brought it to her lips and the hot glass suddenly slipped, dropped to the table, shattered on the floor. She watched horrified as the coffee formed a puddle and the pieces of glass crystallized like islands in a milky brown sea . . .

And then he was there, deftly picking up the glass with his hands and the waiter stood watching, smiling it seemed, while her eyes widened in horror and his only seemed to soften, his honey bear voice in her ear: it's all right, nothing's the matter, everything's fine . . . She looked to the others, surely they would rescue her . . . But everyone was watching, expressions of satisfaction pasted on their mouths, as if witnessing the end of a very good play, the end they'd wanted, foreseen — and his eyes were also on her, his hand on her arm. He gripped it gently or was it firmly? His look was full of devotion or was it cruelty? If she only knew.

Piano

"DO YOU play the piano?" Why did they always say that, when she opened the door and invited them in and they saw the large piano sitting there. Were people's minds really so alike? Did they all think like that? Only once there'd been a man she'd taken home with her, a man she'd met at a dance and kissed as if she'd always known him and wanted him and later when they lay in bed after lovemaking that had not been successful, but which hadn't stopped her from wanting him, he'd said, seeing the piano through the bedroom door, "What do you play?" That was a question she could live with, one with something assumed, something already digested. He was someone she felt sure she could love but he never came back and didn't try to make love to her again after that first clumsy attempt where he'd slipped too quickly in and out of her and she'd said, stupidly, she realized now, "Don't worry. It happens sometimes. It happened with the last man . . ."

Train

HE WAS different from the other ones. The others had laughed, nervously covering their mouths with their hands as she stood, her feet at the edge of the subway platform, her body already leaning into darkness, trying to see light, trying to see — she said — if the train was coming. He pulled her back. "I don't like it," he said, "when you do that." And once on the train, he sat hoping to himself that she would not see the man behind them, the one who kept punching the air with his fist as he paced the car, blustering, spewing expletives; sat hoping he'd exit before she looked up, that she'd continue oblivious, unaware of the craziness that surrounded them. She hadn't, had noticed everyone's eyes turned toward something (someone) in the back. "What is everyone staring at?" And saw for herself the man as he strode the car length, his fist and his words hitting the air with a certain viciousness. "I hadn't wanted you to see . . ." She stared at him; did he really think he could do that . . .? And now as the man neared them he held her arm, as if to pull her away from the shower of words and spit towering over them, to shelter her from any that might fall onto them. "It's okay," she whispered, "You can look up. He's gone now . . ."

Soldier

ONCE SHE had let a soldier in a train compartment love her. She kept this experience in a small tin box with a closed lid. But now without wanting to, she dimly saw the tin box float out of blackness, into view. And once let out, he was difficult to stuff back inside. She saw the army green of his uniform, the bulge at his crotch, milky-brown skin, neat moustache. She felt his hand on her thighs, moving closer. His face . . . she couldn't remember it now. Dark dots of eyes. Eyes she couldn't penetrate, but all the while they seemed to be searching her, stripping her. She felt his hands, an army of ants, invading her body. But it was the uniform — tight and green, clean, pressed — that she couldn't will from her mind. The body it hid so neatly. How quick and furtive he had been. Underneath the tight green cloth desire burned him. She envied his desire, his movements born of need, movements that broke his trappings. Without desire, without need, she had floated to the ceiling of the compartment, watched the soldierman love her. When the train stopped she got off without looking back, without saying a word.

Wine

THEY MOVED, one drunken herd, crashed into closets, bureaus — drawers slid and doors gave way — fell laughing onto the floor and rolled over into the pool of wine they had spilled, let it seep into their clothing and laughing still, removed their clothes, the tangled pant legs, the sweaters over their heads until they lay naked, at first awed by the presence of white skin, and then softly laughed again. And they could not stop laughing. They rolled over and onto each other and then lay, four naked bodies on the wet carpet, waiting for the lamp fixtures to fall, the ceiling to give way, the walls to flatten them.

Café

SHE brushes the hair from her eyes, runs her fingers through it. Driving here she had slowed behind the school bus and watched the morning sun on these bare fields, gently lifting white mist. She had pulled in where the sign dangled from its post, then stood in that lazy streak of sun, where it shaved the sidewalk. She had found this café. Coffee fills hollow spaces. Places where sleep lingers still. She does not think of a man, this man — surveying her distant smile, how her head fits into grey space, just above the right shoulder. He sees grey all around her, a dusty cloak she wears, and the light from the window sifts through the grey. In a moment she will turn, find herself on his clipboard. Glancing up, she meets his expectant eyes. The cup clatters in its saucer. She bites down on her lip. Her fingers run through her hair. She walks briskly to the door. Keeps to the sidewalk's straight edge. There is an echo at her heels, now a breath in her ear, "Madame, you have dropped your smile."

Passenger

I DON'T have to watch the way you unfold the
newspaper, how it rests wide open on your lap, I
don't have to meet the gaze you have fastened to
my shoulder, I have the window — trees stiff as
soldiers, a shallow pond, darkened with leaves —
the way you lay aside that thick newspaper, the
way you cross your thighs languorously doesn't
keep me from staring at the scenery and the slow
stroking of your thigh fingers dragging across
your pant leg doesn't make me turn my head as
you move to sit next to me your body pressing
into mine I don't have to listen to your breath on
my neck too warm a little sweet like baby corn I
don't have to if I don't want to

HOME

Home

EACH TIME she comes home the house looks more cluttered. It's the kitchen that disturbs her — the newspapers stacked on a chair in the corner (now they've reached the chair's height and threaten to spill over), the mail scattered under and on top of the table: letters out of their envelopes, coupons and catalogs, scribbled-on postcards.

She throws it all away. Then wipes the table-cloth until the thread wears through.

She collects the coffee cups — all half-full — washes them one by one. She sweeps the floor until straws break from the broom.

And then she stands. Has she gotten it all? A few things she couldn't tackle: places where the wallpaper has peeled, where linoleum lifts from the counter. Still, it looks good. As a home should.

She opens the refrigerator (she wanted some juice, not too cold, but sweet and good) only to close it again quickly. She had forgotten, not expected to find, what waits within. A task larger than the kitchen. She lifts out jars of soup stock (wilted celery swims inside), of ketchup crusted on the outside. She finds foods she cannot recognize.

She throws it all away. Cleans out the

refrigerator's insides. And then closes the door and closes her eyes.

Her mother arrives soon after. "Oh my daughter you've come home!" She hugs her daughter tightly. Her eyes are bright and her face shines gladly. Only later, when she pulls away, does she notice the room.

She runs her hand along the wall. "What is it?" her daughter asks, but she doesn't answer. Now she goes through the cupboard; cups and bowls clink together. She surveys them on the counter, chooses a grey mug with blue trim.

"Would you like coffee dear?" and she proceeds to make some, letting the coffee grounds spill to the counter, the water run too long in the sink. "Milk?" she asks, and it's then she discovers the refrigerator, and looks with horror at her daughter.

In Bed

B. TELLS me the shoulder pads on the white shirt I'm wearing are showing.

J. has graffiti scars across her forehead; I hardly recognize her.

Two turkeys run by, then two lambs; one bites my hand but not hard enough for it to bleed.

A girl toys with my coat.

A Mexican girl makes love to me, pulling my breasts through my sleeve.

In a theater I sit next to a homeless woman who seems to be masturbating. She tries to rob me as I leave. I struggle for my bag, also for my wallet with the 42 dollars.

I shoot a deer right through with a poisonous arrow.

I lie in bed between my father and mother. A woman flies by on a gigantic, spindly, beautiful bird. Dressed in Guatemalan fabric, she is as multi-colored and as thin as the bird. They look through the garbage pail for food. "Have you looked in S's pail yet?" My mother asks. I feel offended. The garbage is mine, not my sister's.

The woman hovers over us. She gives my father a kiss on the lips and then strums the air above him like a hummingbird. I stare at her, amazed and annoyed. Her parents arrive. My mother and father introduce me, "This is anonymous," they tell them. "Her name is Monica."

17

Letter to My Sister

YESTERDAY I found a door. It opened to a room under the house, one I'd never seen before. The TV was going. I tried to turn it off but none of the knobs would turn. Everything else was made of wood: a crude bed, a desk with papers, and the walls were rough unfinished boards. The bed seemed to take up too much room. It was a real bed, not like my mattress on the floor. It could be mine I thought, and suddenly saw the room transformed; my prints and photographs, my books and shoes sailed down from upstairs. And then I realized. This room would be yours.

Last night I found you sitting with a man on my bed. He was my lover, the latest one. I stood at the door. Wanted to see what went on without me. But suddenly I was speaking, saying something to make him laugh while you watched from the bed.

You are more beautiful than I, and quieter. I am the loud macaw, ruffling up these woodland scenes.

When my relationships fail, I always want to say, as if to bring you out, a part of myself: you'd love my sister more.

But I am growing appendages, like starfish: a new limb where the other severed.

Birthday

THERE WERE hunting dogs on the wallpaper where we sat around a table. The room was dark and the cake was dark chocolate. Her father had thick glasses. Her mother smiled at me, "When will you come again, Rebecca?" "Maybe Rebecca wants to spend the night—wouldn't you like that?" her father said. "My name is Monica," I said into my napkin. I was sweating. I wished they'd stop leaning toward me. "Where's your brother?" I asked her. I wanted to ask where her other friends were, why no one else had come. "He isn't here. He lives in a home," she said. "Maybe Erika would like to meet our boy," her father said. "Wouldn't you like to go to the Home?" "I want to go to my own home," I said. They laughed as if I'd made a big joke. "We like Erika very much, don't we?" her father said. And they nodded with smiles too big for their faces.

Session

HE WAITS until I've finished speaking. "So," he says, "Other people's opinions are very important to you." I nod. My therapist hardly ever says anything; I listen carefully when he does. We have one of our awkward silences then. "Well," he says at last. "That makes you very vulnerable, doesn't it?" I nod before it catches up to me; I haven't really understood what he said. "Why?" I ask. "What do you mean?" He crosses his legs the other way. "Why?" he says, "Because it impacts you." I stare at him. But that's not a word. "Don't you know that's not a word?" I want to ask him. Why is he making it into a verb when it isn't one? "Do you see that?" he says, "Do you see how if affects you?" and I nod very slowly at him.

Dressing Room

THE DRESSING ROOM was small, too small for the two of us. My mother seemed larger than usual, as if she'd grown an extra foot and I had shrunk to accommodate her. I think she had to bend her head not to touch the ceiling, but maybe it was just that I was focusing on her face, the ceiling, so as not to look at the rest of her. She was trying on a two-piece bathing suit, revealing parts of herself I hadn't seen before. The suit was full of green and blue swirls and between the two stretches of cloth was my mother's skin: folds of belly white skin, soft and sagging. Her breasts seemed too large for the suit, and they met above the blue green, creating their own form, a new shape untamed by the material. There was no mirror in the dressing room; you had to step outside to find one and face the eyes of the saleswomen and customers. I knew my mother wasn't going to do that. She stretched and pulled the suit, straightening it around her hips and breasts, "What do you think? Do I look all right? What do you think, Monica?" I wanted her to read my face and see that she looked awful, not at all how my mother should look, that she'd become someone else in it, something grotesque and embarrassing. But she only stared at me, waiting. Why hadn't she chosen one of my sisters, climbed into one of their dressing rooms, stood before them, large and looming?

"How do I look? Should I get it?" "You look nice," I said, swallowing hard, feeling the lie like a lump inside me. Her face showed relief while I felt terrible. My mother looked awful and now, somehow, I was responsible.

Sister

"WHERE'S SOPHIE?" he asks his father. "How come she didn't come?" "Your sister was a bad girl. God changed her into a goldfish," his father says. "A goldfish?" Timothy stares at his father. His father starts to smile, but Timothy has already dropped his father's hand and is backing down the sidewalk in slow steps, before he turns and starts to run. "Timothy!" his father calls after him, but he's too far away to hear. He runs past his mother and her questions, through the kitchen and living room, into the room with the aquarium. There's a new fish, bigger than the others, with long speckled fins that flap as it swims. "Sophie," he says, placing his hands on the glass, "Sophie . . ." and his sister's large fish eyes seem to meet his before his vision blurs.

Visitor

SHE WAKES UP and sees him standing at her door. "Little girl . . ." he says, and his voice is soft and thick like honey, "Ssshh. I'm not going to hurt you . . ." She opens her mouth. She wants to say: Who are you? How did you get into our house? But no sound comes. She sits up and he moves toward her. His hand brushes the hair from her eyes and she feels the tips of his fingers, thick like her father's. He backs away from her. He steps back until he reaches the door and then he's gone, closing it behind him. In the morning she tells them. "It was a dream," her mother says. "You only imagined it," her father says. "No!" she tells them. "No, he was real . . ." But they only shake their heads at her insistence. She looks at her brother. He gets up from the breakfast table and puts on his glasses. "Where are you going?" He doesn't answer. He circles the house slowly. On the pavement he finds a footprint, barely visible, the color of red dust. Red dust: where has he seen it? The print is too big to be his own—too small to be his father's? They watch him carry the left-footed shoes from his father's closet out to the driveway. "What . . .?" "My sister doesn't lie," is all he says.

Motel

WE WERE drinking when he told me: "There was one time, only one, when my Mom tried to leave him. She took us with her—me and my sister, eight and five years old, we went to a Dunkin' Donuts first. She let me drink from her coffee cup and I can remember the way the coffee tasted through the red of her lipstick smudge on the rim and then the squish of the purple jelly in my do-nut—Sus had a chocolate one (I never liked how they tasted). Afterward we made our way to the motel, a plain inexpensive one with checked bed-spreads on trim twin beds (I'll sleep with Sus, Mom said). She had packed a small suitcase for each of us and I rummaged through mine then, just to see what she'd brought—a clean change of clothes, fresh underwear, my comic books and my Matchbox set—and it looked like we'd have a long night of TV with no one to tell us to switch the channel to the news or to turn off the damn thing, Mom wouldn't care, I felt sure of it. But we'd hardly turned down the beds, climbed into the covers and rested our backs against the pil-lows when the phone rang. Stay right where you are! He was coming to get us. 'Mom, how come he knew to call here?' 'It was in the note I left him, I mentioned the name of the motel . . .' I stared at her. So it hadn't been for real after all—

it wasn't even a rehearsal. 'Why did you do that? How could you tell him?' She looked down at her hands propping her up on the bed. 'I don't know . . .' her voice seemed thin. 'I'm sorry, Danny.' I stared at her long and hard, she looked pale and frail sitting on the edge of the bed. But I couldn't pity her, I was too angry. 'Danny, will you forgive me?' Maybe I nodded my head, maybe I said 'yes,' — I don't remember. It didn't really matter, it was over — she'd gone back to being who she'd always been."

Shopping in a
Foreign Country

THE WOMEN surrounded my mother. Shorter
than my mother, they held the dresses on home-
made hangers like banners from an unknown
country above their heads. "*Compreme esto, compreme esto . . . se lo doy barato . . .*" Buy this one from
me, buy this, I'll sell it to you cheap . . .

My mother turned circles, trying to look at
them all, fingering the purple and red embroidery, "This one's nice—so is this . . . I can't
decide—what do you think? You have to help
me . . ." She turned to me to translate, to bar-
gain, to decide for her. The sun reflected off the
white cotton of the dresses; the women's voices
buzzed thick like wasps.

I tried to be precise, authoritative. "What about
this one—blue and pink look good on you . . ."

"Do you think so? But I need one for my sister
too . . . Ask her how much it is."

Each time my mother grew near to deciding,
another woman cut in front of her, tugging at her,
asking her to feel the quality of material, to examine the embroidery, while another woman cut in
front of her, "*Señora, compreme esto, compreme
esto . . . Señora, se lo doy mas barato, Señora . . .*"

"But I can't buy them all . . ." my mother said,

"I'm not rich . . . Tell them that I'm not rich, Monica, I can't possibly buy every one . . ."

"You don't have to. Just choose," I said, "Just choose one, Mom," my voice sharper, colder, as my mother's weakened and wavered.

"I don't know . . . the rest will feel bad. Who should I give the money to? Which do I choose?" Her voice edged toward tears.

"The one you want, Mom, get the one you want," irritated that she shouldn't know which one that was.

"I don't know . . ." The tears came to her eyes, "Help me choose, Monica."

I chose the same blue and pink one I'd decided on earlier; a red, purple, and black one for her sister. My mother gave me her wallet and I counted out the bills for her, paid the two women who quickly slipped the dresses from their stick hangers to give to her. The rest dropped theirs to their sides, still watching. They smiled shyly.

"*Pobrecita*," one said, "Poor little one," and she reached her arms around my mom. The others followed, each taking a turn to clasp my mother to her smaller, shorter self, laughing as they did, until my mother and I laughed too, "*Pobrecita, pobrecita* . . ." we said.

The Women of Nijar

THEY ARE driving; that is, their mother is driving. Their father isn't with them; he's in the States on business — their mother has said he's looking for a job. She's decided to take them to Nijar, a place she's heard about, a town where women carry clay pots on their heads.

There are three of them: the eldest daughter, the middle child and the youngest, a son.

It's getting darker. This is the corner of Spain where the desert meets the ocean. The road leads inland, away from the coast, farther into the mountains, and the mountains, dry and somber, seem to be swallowing the road. They haven't passed another car; they haven't seen a town; in fact, it seems to all of them, though it hasn't been said, that even the road will cease to exist soon.

The car, a VW van bought by their father in Germany, seems hollow and tinny as it plows over ruts and stones in the road. They feel like its contents, things that have sprung loose and are rattling and bumping against one another. They endure the bumping and the rattling without saying anything until the oldest of them, after her head almost scrapes the ceiling, says, "Are you sure this place exists?"

"Of course it does," their mother says.

And then for a while no one says anything.

29

"Do you think it's the right road?" the boy asks. Even though he's the youngest, only nine, without his father he feels responsible.

"Well, it was the only one, wasn't it? There wasn't any other," their mother says.

The oldest is squinting her eyes at the road. She needs glasses, though she doesn't want to admit this. She's trying to see ahead as far as she can, trying to foresee the possibility of a town.

"I don't see why we're looking for it anyway," she says finally.

"Don't you want to see the women?" her sister asks, but she only shrugs.

"What do they carry in those pots anyway?" the boy asks.

They wait for their mother to answer but she seems not to have heard them.

"Water," the younger sister says. "They carry water. Right, Mom? And they don't spill anything even though they have to walk barefoot uphill." She sees them: women in long skirts with tall cylindrical pots resting on their heads. They scurry away as the car approaches, one hand reaching up to steady their pots. She sees them like the ants in an anthill she once stumbled on, darting in all directions at once, a flurry of color: their purple and red skirts flapping after them. It must be a beautiful thing or why would their mother take them so far to see it? Something beautiful but difficult to get to, like the beach she found with her brother at the foot of a steep cliff with no path to climb down on. A beach with speckled white sand and huge rocks that had holes in them.

The oldest is biting her nails; her brother and sister have their faces pressed against the window. There isn't much to see: a landscape without trees, lots of cacti and the barbed shrubs that seem to grow everywhere. Back there they passed an old well, the kind a donkey is used to haul water from, trudging slowly around while attached to a wooden pole, but there was no donkey.

They passed the well without saying anything, but now they're thinking about it. It must have gone dry, the boy thinks. There's so little water here — besides the ocean — it doesn't seem like a landscape meant for people and animals. A good thing I brought my canteen and jackknife, he thinks. If we get stuck, what will we live on? Cactus? He's heard they're a good source of water. Once he and his sisters tried a prickly pear, squeezing the water into their mouths, not the way you should do it, he supposed, because it left invisible prickers on their tongues and lips; for hours they were trying to pull out the tiny hairs.

"I don't think we're going to find that town," he says suddenly.

"I don't either," the oldest quickly adds. "Let's go back now, Mom."

"But it has to be around here somewhere," their mother says, "There's no other road it could be on . . ."

"Well, maybe we took a wrong turn somewhere," the boy says.

"But where? We couldn't have. Just a few more miles. I know it's here, according to the map, it's just around the next bend."

"Mom, it isn't even *on* the map," the oldest says.

They wait for their mother to contradict her. But she doesn't say anything. She keeps her eyes on the road. She starts to hum a song, the tail end of some tune, then stops herself. It's true it isn't on the map. But neither are a lot of towns, including the one they've been living in for almost a year. But she says nothing. It will only aggravate them further. Best not to say anything, sometimes. Perhaps she should turn around. If her husband were here, he'd do that now. But they've already come so far—it makes no sense now. If they turn around, they'll miss it. She knows they won't drive out this way again.

The air is deep blue and darkening. They can see the moon now, a thin shadow of itself, suspended over the mountains.

Where is their father now? They don't think about him, have accepted his absence without questioning. Only sometimes at night they imagine his return, with presents for each of them and stories of back home, a place that appears less and less real, more and more fantastic—where all good things abound, where trees and hills are soft and green, not like the countryside here, dry and dusty, with plants tangled and prickly, where only what's sharp or venomous can survive.

They do not think about their father, but his absence is with them, an undefined space, a black hole growing larger, absorbing more room in the car. They sense their mother is unsure, uncertain where she is taking them, though it is clearly pictured in her mind: rows of white plaster houses built into the hillside, the blue of the sky against the white plaster . . . A little plaza, a fountain with a garden. And the women: majestic, upright, their pots brimming over with water, eyes dark and defiant . . . She'd like to take photographs. It's getting awfully dark. Did she bring her flash? It's not the same with flash though.

They complain to her now, "Let's turn back now, Mom . . . it's getting darker . . ." except for the younger sister, who has absorbed her mother's picture, "But the women—don't you want to see the women?"

"We'll give it twenty more minutes," their mother persuades them, "If we haven't come to a town by then, we'll go on home." She wonders at her own determination. She is determined to find it and yet her own doubt is surfacing, carving out space in her mind: What if it is all a joke after all? She remembers the snails, a gift from Maria and Salvador who run the Bar-café in their village. They told her how to prepare them. She cooked them with the garlic and tomato sauce but they were hard and tasteless: like rubber erasers, her children had said, and refused to eat them. She made them anyway, told them they had to eat

33

three each; she couldn't stand for food to be wasted, especially now, when poverty surrounded them.

Later she complained to Paca, her cleaning woman. "Didn't you soak them?" Paca said. "You have to soak them for 48 hours. They have to get rid of their *basurita*, their little garbage," she added. But no one had told her. And once she'd been give n an octopus—they gave it to her in a pot of water. She put it in the back of the car and told her son to watch it while they drove home. "Mom!" he shouted before they'd gone half a kilometer, "It squirted black stuff! It's all black now!" It had let go of its ink; she thought it must be poisoned now.

Or the cuttlefish they were always giving her: a fish that was more bone than flesh; a bone like a surfboard, her children said.

She thought the village was conspiring against her. Maybe Paca, too, even though she paid her a good wage, even though she gave her the clothes her son had outgrown for Juanito, the same age as her own but much smaller-boned.

So Nijar's just another joke. She can feel her eyes smarting. Why do they hate her? Why all these tricks on her?

"Look, Mom!" they shout suddenly, "A town! There's a town!"

The dirt road has turned abruptly and the car lurches forward onto an empty square. She stops the car in front of a pile of stones. There are a few

houses, dark with doors and shutters closed, surrounding the square.

They're silent for a moment, waiting.

"It's ugly here," the oldest says.

"Is this it, Mom?" the boy asks.

She doesn't answer. An old man appears suddenly; they can't tell from where.

Their mother rolls the window down. "¿Es-
tamos en Nijar?" she asks him in her American-
sounding Spanish.

The man stares. He doesn't say anything. One
eyebrow seems to rise slightly, but they aren't
sure they see this.

"This must be it," she says, starting up the
motor.

"But the women—where are the women?"

She circles once around the square, pulling
onto the road they drove in on.

"It's late now. We must have missed them," she
says.

"But Mom! Can't we at least look around?"

"I don't think so, it's almost dark now . . ."

"But Mom . . ."

She keeps on driving.

"All that driving to get nowhere and then just
turn around—kind of a waste of time . . ." the
oldest says. Suddenly it all seems so pointless to
her—why did her mother ever take them here?

Her brother and sister sit with their disap-
pointment. Because who knows—since they
haven't looked around—what might be hiding

there, on the road that forked off, the one their mother ignored. Maybe the white houses lay up that road, the women standing just inside their open doors . . .

Their mother can feel their resistance as she pushes homeward, it fills the car, but her own sense of defeat is stronger, pressing her on and her anger at the villagers, at herself for believing them, for thinking they were on her side —who is on her side after all? Isn't she alone, with her husband across the ocean, with no letter from him yet and no calls because they have no phone —

"Mom, look—what's that?" the boy asks.

They follow where he's pointing with their eyes, see a small column of black moving slowly along the base of the mountain, heading toward the town.

"The women! They're the women!" the youngest sister says. "They're going home. Do you see? And they're carrying pots!"

"No, they're not!" her sister says.

"They're pack horses, aren't they, Mom?"

"But I can see the pots, can't you see them on their heads —there, in a line, big tall ones!"

They strain to see once more, their faces pressed against the glass, then settle back in the quiet of the car, listening to the motor hum — those weren't any pots, were they? Isn't their sister imagining things? In the dark they can't really tell, but the mountains look more and more like velvet with night settling down among them.

36

ZAMORA

El Zacatecano

THAT'S HIM there, and look, Julio is with him —
the one he lives with. That's their home — see the
letters painted on the front, as zig-zaggy as the Z
in Zacatecas. Zacatecas where he was born,
where he traveled from . . . from that steep town
to this one, sprawled across the valley, spreading
every day farther, held in only by the valley air so
thick and white it must be hiding something.
Look, he's setting up shop now. Julio looks on
sleepily, knowing every motion of this early
morning routine. From under the red wagon El
Zacatecano brings out the folding chair, the red
box with the black lid. He sits now in the chair,
and opening the box, lifts out the jar of black, of
brown, of royal blue. He keeps the red in the box,
for these days it goes unrequested, but he knows
as well as anyone that times are prone to change.
He brings out the various colored rags, the deer-
skin cloth, the one for the final shine. He whistles
a foggy tune, one he can't remember where he
found, and Julio looks up, alerted. From his po-
sition (forelegs forward, hindlegs bent, chin resting on the pavement) he has the best view in the
world of the city's shoes. Sandals, sneakers, loaf-
ers, oxfords, boots of rubber and boots of leather,
heels, platforms, flats: though he doesn't know
their names he knows which ones need shining.

He singles them out from the parade, thumping his tail while eyeing them fixedly. El Zacatecano catches Julio's gaze and follows it. Oh the grey leather showing through! The dusty tips! The mud-spattered sides of shoes! And you as you walk past find the condition of your shoes written into their gaze. You steal a downward glance, hesitate, turn back as if you'd suddenly remembered what you'd forgot, then sit to offer up your feet, your humble shoes. And look, others too have glanced downward, looked where their feet walked, turned back for the crouched man and the dog who lies beside him.

Janitzio

AN ISLAND has its own logic, its own rules. You cannot follow them, you can only watch, surrounded. This island seems like another I once explored; only the inhabitants differ. On that other island they were birds that flocked and swarmed and ran circles round me. Here, children.

The island is a small mountain, someone's elbow, a clumpy pyramid. Perhaps you have been there too. Then you know its inhabitants. The island is their playground. Their mothers stay in the cool dark of their white-washed homes. You can see them through the filmy curtain at the door, in the room lined with night, eyes swimming in the dark. Others catch you at the road with their tables of food. The fathers stay behind houses, with tobacco in their gums and between teeth, spitting now and then. Had you come earlier, at the mornings's first light, you would have seen them on the lake, with nets larger than their boats.

But it's afternoon now. Everyone's on the island and only its children can be seen. They watch you. You of a different land, with the scent of money still on your hands. A land they've seen from afar only. Long and flat, not favored by the sun as theirs, that bends toward the light as a

41

plant does. They watch you, your hands in your pockets, fingering the magic. They know its power. Their mothers and fathers have shown them with eyes that shine. They have learned to perform for it, to make offerings, to sing. One exchanges one thing for this other.

This is how their fathers receive it. With white fish caught from the lake. This the lake gives to their fathers. This is how their mothers receive it, with offerings of rich food: the cooked white fish, with tamales, *atole*, *charales*.

Some days magic is scarce, too little to go around even on this small island. Women have to scream above the others: ¡PESCADO BLANCO! ¡CHARALES! ¡RICOS TAMALES! ¡ATOLE...! The children run to the boats, to be the first to greet the bearers of magic, the first to sing to you, the first to exchange candy, postcards, and gum. They follow you noisily.

You climb up the steep path, a trickle of dry brook bed. They climb up after you. You rest and one is singing for you: *Flor de Canela*, Cinnamon Flower. This time you have no coins in your pockets, but a bag of peanuts, bought on the mainland.

The boy with the dark skin pulls on his shorts and sings. He stares at one place only, so as not to forget his lines: Cinnamon flower, how sweet you smell, how sweet are the memories of my loved one . . . He is staring at your bag of peanuts. He sings as fixedly as he stares, without modulation

42

of voice, without melody; he chants in the manner of his ancestors. He has finished, swallowed his last word. His eyes still fixed on the bag in your hand.

You give him a fistful. But your fist is bigger than his. Some peanuts drop to the ground. The other children grab them. Your singer wants to cry. You take back the peanuts, he pulls his shirt out, you place them there. Still holding the corners of his shirt, his feet sing as he runs.

The others grind the dirt with their toes, look up at you hopefully. They've practiced no songs, only long glances, sad, mournful, with eyes that plead darkly.

You give them but one each and climb upward. Another boy has found you. He stands apart from the others. Older perhaps, tougher. His shirt has holes. His pants without a zipper. He has a song about *La Suegra*, the mother-in-law: When my mother-in-law dies, I'll bury her face down, so if she tries to escape, she'll just go down farther... He sings as the other boy did, as his mother does, as his ancestors have; he chants, his voice rising and falling with the words, not the melody. Through time and conquests the songs have changed, but the manner of singing—a deeper, darker knowledge, the thing that cannot be conquered, learned, unlearned—persists.

His song finishes in the same tone it was started, the same tone it was sung; only his mouth dropping shut tells you it's the end. You give him a fistful of peanuts. He takes them in both hands and runs off, not dropping a single one. You give the others but one each, your faithful followers.

The summit is the only flat part of the island. The children running circles round you, the steep trek to the water below make you dizzy. You rest on the stone ledge; the green blue of the lake steadies you.

¿Canto La Suegra? Still another boy, the same song. I've already heard that one, you tell him. Sing another. He looks at you, confused. His eyes drop to your bag of peanuts. It's obvious he knows only one song. Only two have found the island and stayed, circulated faithfully by the island's children: *La Suegra* and *Flor de Canela*.

You settle for *La Suegra*. The boy, smaller than the other two, so skinny his shorts have nothing to hang onto, rushes through the song. He sings in a small mushroom voice. Hey little fellow, louder, I can't hear you. You bend down. He is whispering. His eyes on the peanuts. You've caught but one word from the long litany: *la suegra*. You give him a fistful. He walks away, his free hand holding up his shorts.

You've only a few peanuts left. You distribute no more to those who follow you as you trudge the dirt road winding down the other side. The road is lined with houses. From every house springs a child. Un peso! Un peso! You keep walking. A girl, larger than the rest, plants herself in front of you. *Un peso! Déme un peso!* Her voice is shrill, like the red of her dress. You give her the last of the peanuts; she grabs them greedily and runs, disappearing into the cave of her house. You see her mother there, rising from the dark.

You wonder why you settled on that particular girl for the last of your donations. Something in the sharpness of her voice, her eyes. Challenging you.

You make your way down. Your followers have lost interest. The clump of boys dissolves into two and three and four. They dwindle behind you, walking backward. Watching still.

It's almost dark now. The sun is setting, diffused at the rim of the lake. You've nearly reached your boat. But there's one more beggar boy. He has no legs but moves by the palms of his hands. He swings out, crablike, to your feet, holds out his palm. His eyes do not reproach. Asking only. But you've nothing left to give.

In the Bar-Café

HE GREETED us as if he knew, had expected our arrival. Stretched his hands forward —they were twisted or on backwards: his left hand on his right arm. He winked at me and brought us both a glass of wine. *"¡Para Ustedes! ¡Para Ustedes!"* he said and clinked our glasses and drank the wine. He called to the bartender for sardines, *"¡tres sardinas picantes!"* "Ah!" he said, relishing them with his eyes: three spiced-red fish. He took one by the tail and dangled it from his strange contorted hand. He caught it in his mouth, smiling as he watched me from the corner of his eye. He motioned us to do the same. We hesitated before the plate of fish, but he pushed   us toward it. "It's for you, for you," he insisted with his eyes. I brought the fish to my mouth and the man leaned toward me. I swallowed and felt him close and then his lips touched mine. A violent shiver ran down my spine. *"¡Deliciosa!"* He laughed, his shoulders murmured, and his hands fluttered like unleashed birds.

The Oaxacan Mushroom

HER MOTHER embarrassed her: the black cape
she wore, the hair she didn't comb. Their house
was dark, the plants overgrown. Sometimes her
mother was gone for long days and Rocio was left
alone with the plants, the candles, herbs, and jars
of water. She was left with instructions only:
change the water in the water jars, light new candles, burn incense nightly. Rocio followed the instructions diligently, afraid not to.

At night she felt the plants surrounding her,
saw herself in a jungle, a place her mother had
described but never shown her. Leaves, shining
green, spread out like a canopy over her. She
heard the whirring of insects, an orchestra in the
leaves. A warm breeze, smelling like sweat, as if
just wafted in off a man's hairy chest, blew over
her. Candles flickered like fireflies. She fell to
dreaming, woke up sweating, fell asleep again.

Her mother returned a few days later. She
brought Rocio a small bunch of gardenias, their
petals thick and pale yellow. That she'd bought
them from an Indian in a marketplace was all her
mother told her. They smelled so sweet and rich
that Rocio wanted to bury her face in them. She
held them and imagined other worlds, fragrant
yellow and satin.

"You're going to kill those flowers," her mother

told her, and they did die, just as her mother said. Their petals browned like tobacco stains; they no longer smelled. She wanted a gift she could keep always, that wouldn't wither or die. She told this to her mother. "All right," her mother said. "I'm going away again, I'll see what I can find."

She came back with a mushroom. She'd carried it all the way from Oaxaca by train. It was kept in a dish of tea water; she changed the tea every evening at nine. The mushroom fed on the tea, had grown large and gelatinous and floating, had filled the entire dish (they grow as large as the receptacle they're placed in, her mother said) and would reproduce in time. "For the reproduced mushroom," her mother said, "you will give me one hundred pesos in coins. And then we shall wait for the mothering mushroom to turn to dust, and keep this dust in a pouch, and with it, good luck and prosperity shall come in all things."

The mushroom was kept in the bathroom. Rocio sensed its presence each time she entered the room. She felt compelled to look in the dish, to note its progress. It floated grey, like jellyfish, only more mucilaginous; it made her shudder and close her eyes. But in darkness she felt it grow still more, and had to look again, to see her fears confirmed.

What was to keep it in the dish? Wouldn't it grow still larger, mounting the dish's sides? She felt it would stop only at the bathroom walls. She waited for it to reproduce and felt relieved to imagine the mushroom as dust, a fine powder, nothing slimy, slippery, slithery about it.

How could she tell her mother that her gift repelled her, that she'd imagined something else, something more beautiful. She saw the pleasure it gave her; she heard her singing fragments of songs as she brewed a new batch of tea. She'd call Rocio over to admire it, "Look, it's grown a bit more, can you see? It's a perfect specimen . . . I wonder when it will have its child?" And Rocio would observe it obediently, swallowing her apprehension. "But isn't it taking awfully long?" she once asked her. "Oh no, I don't think so," her mother said, carefully pouring out the brown tea water and replacing it with a darker batch, "These things take time. One must be patient always . . . Life is often a matter of waiting," and stood, admiring it once more.

At night Rocio could feel it grow larger. She'd lie still, sensing its night movement. It seemed to feed on the dark, the color of tea, on the moistness of the bathroom. And everything took on its gelatinous aspect: the towels, hanging damply in a line, the soap in its slimy soap dish, the floor of the shower, kept wet by a drippy faucet, looking translucent in the light of the moon.

Rocio hid beneath her covers, tried to imagine things dry and dusty, the desert in Sonora her mother had once taken her to see, the ash from incense, grey powder magically still in the shape of a cone, the dusty bodies and stiff wings of insects that died on windowsills, the one she'd found in the sugarbowl (had the sugar killed it?) or the mushroom itself—now dust, like the volcanic ash her mother kept in a jar, without color, odor, life . . .

In the morning she realized she had not willed it to powder. It was there, larger, lapping the side of the bowl; as if to an invisible tide, a pattern of its own, it undulated and lolled. During the day she dismissed it; she concentrated on school. Biology reassured her with its experiments and diagrams. She saw that nature could be managed, maneuvered, or controlled. If only her mother knew.

But at night knowledge receded. She heard the mushroom lapping, overlapping the bowl, filling the bathroom, reflecting the moon . . . She covered her eyes. But she found it where she turned—under her pillow, in the sheets, slipping between her toes. Until she decided she must face the root of her fear, and trembling but determined, went into the bathroom.

Her mother, hearing a scream, rushed for her daughter. She found her, looking awful in the dim light, standing over the toilet. The water gurgled down. She noticed too, the mushroom dish in pieces on the floor.

"My Oaxacan mushroom!" her mother gasped. "One of Maria Sabina's own . . ."

Rocio stood, trembling still, unable to face her mother.

"Oh Rocio, how could you?"

"It was an accident . . ."

"Accident or no—it's an evil omen. Quickly, come into the living room."

Rocio followed numbly. She knelt where her mother told her to. She watched her mother's movements, flickering like the candles she lit in the dark room. She held out her hand to receive one hundred pesos in coins.

"You must bury these, outside in a place—don't tell me—do it quickly but do it well, not in a shallow grave, a deep one—go on, hurry!"

Rocio carried the coins in her outstretched palms as if sleepwalking. In a patch near the garden she began to dig with her fingers, digging quickly, feeling the dirt, cold in her fingernails, thinking vaguely that she hadn't killed the mushroom at all. Wouldn't it continue to grow, enlarging and enlarging, filling the pipes and tanks below, reproducing too—what was to stop it?

Her fingers worked rapidly; she placed the coins in the hole. She flung the dirt on top of them. But it wasn't enough. They needed more. She couldn't seem to work quickly enough. She dug and filled, dug and filled, feeling all the while it was senseless, and her mother must know that too; they couldn't be buried well.

Zamora

HE JERKED awake. The conductor was calling out his destination. Quickly he stood up, straightening his suit as he did so, and pulled his valise from the overhead rack.

"Excuse me," he said hurriedly, somewhat insistently, to the passenger beside him. The passenger was reading a newspaper. His legs were crossed and one foot jutted into the aisle, blocking the man's way. Without looking up from his newspaper, he slowly uncrossed his legs.

"Thank you," the man muttered, and hurried down the aisle. He jumped off the train just as it was pulling away from his destination.

The sun was bright after the dark interior of the train, the station, empty. The man, still clutching his valise and hat to his chest, blinked his eyes.

The station seemed different than he remembered it. Perhaps it was only the white paint. Funny how a coat of paint can change a place entirely, like a pair of new pants can a man. He walked past the solid cement benches: sentinels guarding empty tracks. There was an air of the unfamiliar. The man squinted his eyes as if to make it recognizable.

He checked his watch. He had some time before his meeting. He realized he still held his hat in his hands. He placed it on his head, and with his valise in one hand, continued walking.

How strangely quiet the place was. For a moment he wondered if he'd gotten off at the wrong station. He looked behind him for the sign on the station wall, the famil iar black letters, just to be sure. The wall stared back at him, a blank white stare. Perhaps the sign had been painted over, and the letters had still to be painted on. But he felt disconcerted. He recalled the conductor's voice, confident, controlled: Zamora, he had called. And again: ZAMORA, with more resonance the second time. And he had woken, as if it had been his own name the conductor had spoken.

He walked along the dirt road. The sun glanced off the white plaster houses. He had the address of his meeting written on the back of his ticket stub. He pulled the stub from his pocket, reading the address aloud: 37 Progreso Street. He looked around for a street sign, and noticed the intersection farther ahead. But the intersection indicated neither the name of the street he was on, nor the one which crossed it. And yet, this other street, running perpendicular, did seem to have a familiar tone: its white houses, the view from where he stood . . . Hadn't he seen it before? With new determination, he turned down the road.

How hot it was! He stopped for a moment to remove his hat and wipe his brow. And yes, he thought, I'm wearing the wrong clothes. Then remembered it was a meeting he was attending. Only a suit would do. He wondered now if he'd brought the right papers. Sitting down on a stone in the road, he unclasped his valise. He shifted his weight to get comfortable, then pulled out a folder and the envelopes he'd stuffed inside.

Overhead a plane went by. The man jumped up, waving frantically, then slowed his arm. Now what did I do that for? He shrugged. Oh the heat. It was really too hot. He let his hat fall from his hands and it rested with the contents of his valise, which had scattered when he stood to flag the plane. He removed his jacket and slung it over his arm.

"Odd," he muttered to himself, and continued walking. He approached the next intersection cautiously. Now what was the name of that street he wanted? He searched his pockets for the ticket stub. I must've dropped it, he thought, for there was nothing there. He pulled out the lining, just to make sure, letting his jacket slide from his arm.

"Oh the heat!" The sun seemed to be glaring now, blinding him from the white plaster houses it trapped and burnished. With one hand he shielded his eyes, muttering, "There's got to be a sign. I've only to find it." But wait. Wasn't that something ahead? A kind of post, some painted words?

He stumbled forward and circled slowly, carefully, all senses alert, like a police dog, detecting. A letter . . . part of a word, was all he wanted. He stopped suddenly. A rumbling in the distance . . . the train? But was that the sound a train made? He tried to recall, to pull out his rack of sounds, words, sensations. He fumbled mentally. But already the sound had lost its familiar edge. Memory had left him.

Translations

THAT MORNING we walked past houses of mud, red windowsills, flower pots, grass soaked green. Crossed a small bridge we should not have looked over but did, saw garbage choking a small stream, and a dog pawing the water, the floating trash, as if to climb upstream or looking for his meal — soaked, sinking now. Dogs fend for themselves here, I explained. I was explaining everything we saw, or thought you saw. We passed women with buckets of water. So much unnecessary labor, you remarked. A man tying a rope with wife, son; staking out his territory, you surmised. I had left off explaining, translating: foreigners both now. The town, so picturesque, neat, red-and-white-clean far behind, the stares longer, the skin darker, but the houses still with their insides barred. We on the outside (did you see the gardens through the doors?) making phrases for what we saw. I wanted to tell you not this but about the lover and the loved one, thought I could put it neatly: I dislike being the one who is loved. But later in the hotel when you came to me, pale skin yellow shirt (mud brown and green gone now) put your lips to mine, I still had not told you and had to struggle out of the tangle of words, thoughts, your arms.

The Other Direction

SHE LEFT the house, closing the door behind her. Walked the other way down the street. Not toward the market, the small and various stores — shapes of papaya and mango in one, buckets, nails, rows of red cloth in others. She crossed the large avenue, threading her way through cars, arrows shooting past her. She walked in the direction she had no reason to go.

Buildings huddled together, houses that remained closed to her. A man stood in the doorway, calling after her.

"*Mamacita*, come inside with me . . ."

She remembered the man she left sleeping.

She passed the morning sweeper, broom of bundled sticks, stepped over his pile of dirt and wrappings. Eyes followed her. She felt their warnings but kept on walking.

A woman stooped to dump a pail of dishwater. Paused with her emptied bucket to stare. Eyes less revealing than the man's, something closeted.

She walked past the stick trees with few leaves, grown from scratches in the dirt. The dirt was grey and lifeless. It swallowed the road and then the sidewalk. She followed it.

Buildings lost all color. Nor did any cars pass her. She stepped around a sleeping dog, his mangy fur pulled tightly over him.

She remembered the man she left sleeping. She

saw him like a dream. Now he reached for her. He rolled onto the empty side of bed. The dust swept in her eyes. She rubbed them and tasted salt and soot mingled in.

She passed a small boy making lines with a shard of red brick. He pulled the brick after him, carving a single line through the dirt. It turned corners and zig-zagged in places; she followed. No houses stood there. The line continued.

She remembered the man in a dream; he was calling after her. She thought she heard her name, but it was only the sound of the line, scraped through dirt. Her name held no sound, no syllables to roll on her tongue, only letters, themselves like lines.

The piece of brick had crumbled to bits. The boy held them out to her. She took the crumbled brick, feeling its color in the palm of her hand.

The line continued no farther. She felt it behind her. Fingernails scraped through dirt. She pushed the dirt with the toe of her shoe. A thicker line of her own making. She plowed forward, walked, plowed then walked, until ahead of her was the familiar, and behind her; she didn't know.

NIGHT

Night

SHE WOKE UP during the night. She thought she'd heard barking but it was only a dream: she was with him again. They were making love, breathing so hard they didn't notice his dog until he was standing over them, barking fiercely. But how could she dream what had already happened? In movies too, watching a couple in bed, she suddenly saw herself and him while his black dog, confused at the noisy animal they'd become, barked at them. She closed her eyes and pulled the blanket tightly around her; she was shivering.

In Higher Altitude

HE HAD invited her to his room once. She thought she shouldn't but knew she'd go. They started to walk there. And then suddenly he remembered he was to have been somewhere half an hour ago. He kissed her on the cheek and was gone. That was the last time she saw him.

Sometimes she thinks it went like that. Other times she sees his room: dark, wood-panelled, a Persian rug, a messy bed. She sat on his bed, surveying the room. He rented it from a Marxist filmmaker. He was showing her things — photos he had taken, a book of poems a friend had written. They went up to the roof to take his clothes off the line. The sky was steel-grey, menacing. She shivered. He was wearing shorts, long and baggy. He always did. Even in New York City in the winter. At least that's what he said. His cotton shirts flapped in the wind. She took them down one by one, folded them neatly. They went to his room again. He was nervous, pacing the room, talking about his ex-girlfriend and her new lover. He sat down beside her and said he wanted to make love. They did. She never saw him again.

Or she sees herself in the café where she first met him. She had arrived later than usual. It occurred to her that he'd come and left already. She looked around nervously. She called the waiter for coffee. He handed her a folded piece of paper.

It was a note from him. Remember what I said about keeping a distance with people I love. Or something like that. She doesn't remember exactly. She'd ripped it into small pieces, dropped it in her coffee.

Sometimes she dreams about him. She wakes confused. She feels her husband must know she hasn't spent the night with him. He asks her how she slept. She answers but her eyes avoid his.

She is sitting in the café; she goes there still. She keeps looking toward the door; its small bell disturbs her. She has a book but she can't concentrate. The words seem to be written in another language, one she hasn't mastered.

She remembers meeting him. She'd see him across the café reading from that thick book of his, laughing aloud. She meant to tell him to control his outbursts of laughter; he looked like a young version of a crazy old man. She thought she would, eventually. First, she'd ask him what the book was. She couldn't tell from where she was. Suddenly he was standing before her. She hadn't seen him approaching. She thought he'd ask for matches. He asked for a piece of paper instead. She tore one from her notebook. It ripped and she had to start again. He stood looking at her. Will you be here tomorrow so I can borrow more paper? She laughed and said she would.

His eyes were electric light blue. She loved to watch them. In a land where men were short and dark-skinned, he looked different. There was something tense in his eyes and his hair, curly red, something that riveted her to him. Sometimes when he spoke he grabbed her arm, as if he knew she hadn't the same intensity, that she might not be hearing what he said, but thinking about what she saw. Once their knees touched under the table and he told her not to move—it felt good, he was cold (in shorts only), until she couldn't concentrate, feeling even that knobbiest part of his body against her. And then he stood up, pulled on his sweater; he remembered he had to be somewhere.

He was only 19. She remembers herself at 19. Would they have fallen in love had they met then? She thinks they would have. Better that she met him older and married; she had her defenses.

She sees the man in the blue blazer at the back of the café, the one he said was following him. He seems to be watching her. But that's crazy. No one is following him, or her. He had his paranoia she had no part in. Only recently she'd noticed a car, large, sleek, maroon; she found it parked where the bus let her off at the curb. It seemed to be following her. She'd counted three times now. But this was crazy. Yet she wanted to tell him. He thrived on such stories. He'd want to go with her, take his camera; he'd dare to run up to the window and photograph the driver.

He had lived out his paranoia one winter in an apartment alone. He cracked all the windows, watched the glass splinter. He broke them from the inside, listened to the glass shatter on the pavement below. The wind blew in cold. He photographed the empty windows, the bed, his books, every object in the room. He pasted the photographs on the walls. He photographed these too. He placed everything along the walls. He piled them in the center, in patterns on the floor. Arranging, rearranging. He'd stare at himself in the mirror. He'd hear knocking. He'd comb his hair, trying to rearrange this disorder that was himself, his room, his mind. He prepared a smile, what he was going to say. The knocking grew louder. He threw the door open. No one was there.

Don't be afraid of being sane, she had told him. But that was like death to him. This way he was different, apart, saved from almost everyone. Mentally unstable, his mother had said. She hated him, he said.

Sometimes lying next to her husband in bed she worried about him. He was alone; it was not his city. He said he came for the altitude. It's true high altitude makes you visionary, he had said. Once when making love to her husband she had seen him instead, saw his laughter, his smile, saw that these were lying to her. She felt his loneliness, a balloon of sadness he carried with him carefully hidden, so it didn't prick and burst open. Pricks of sadness like needles, needling him. Perhaps her husband knew she wasn't with him; he turned to curl away from her.

Last night her husband hadn't come home. Lying in bed she saw another room, small and dark and carpeted. She had his phone number. Tell me if you're going to call, I never answer. She let it ring and ring, into the darkness of the house she imagined. She felt grateful for the telephone; it was persistent, relentless in a way she could never be. But no one answered.

It was 3 A.M. She didn't know where her husband was. She thought she should be worried. Or angry. Jealous even. She tried to find the word to name her feelings. It wasn't one of these. She went to bed, woke when he came in. Where were you? Her voice accused him. With friends . . . I went out drinking with friends. She didn't say anything. Are you angry at me? She closed her eyes.

She tries to picture her husband. His face is still beautiful. A face that has always made her want to touch him: the pure skin, high cheeks, his long eyelashes. She sees these, but they don't fit into one picture; she sees only his eyes, then his ears, the back of his hair. She tries hard to see his face all in one, to hold onto the picture.

Her head hurts from all the coffee. She hears the bell like some ringing in her head. She thinks of ordering a sandwich. She used to order one just so he'd take a bite from hers. He doesn't eat.

He lives on nervous energy, fueled by coffee and cigarettes, espresso and non-filter.

She sees him come in, his curly red head, his blue eyes laughing. He sits at a table across the room. She stares into her coffee. She waits for him to see her. He doesn't come. She feels stung by him. Do you think I am following you? She asks him silently. She looks at him for an answer. He stares back. He has a moustache. It isn't him.

The man in the blue blazer is leaving. Wait, she says. The man turns toward her. Did she really say that? She looks away from him. She feels her mouth tightening. They are sweeping the café. Chairs sit upside down on tables, their heads hanging. She hears the bell ringing, but no one is entering.

She looks for something he'd given her, a scrap of paper with his handwriting, anything. There had been a note — the writing long and jagged, capital and small letters jumbled together — she *had* read it, hadn't she? Then torn it in pieces . . . She can't remember exactly. She finds his telephone number. But the numbers are clear, distinct. She'd copied it down from him. You fool, she says. She hears the phone ringing in his apartment, dark and empty. She tries to remember if she'd been there once, with him. Had she only imagined it — the house, the note, him?

Her head is pounding. She makes her way through the tables with chairs. She opens the door and the cool air catches her. The air feels thin.

One Thing

THERE WAS one thing she hadn't told him. Of course there must be others, lots of things. But this one thing . . . She thought she could tell him; she would tell him now: there was a time I was so afraid that I lived like a rabbit . . . No, she couldn't bring herself—something always stopped her. Instead she'd remember the time, the place: a farmhouse, long ago abandoned, without furniture, with plaster crumbling walls.

She comes to sleep there. In the loft where green shoots poke through cracks in the wood. Next to the wall where moss grows. Night comes in through open windows. Outside trees creak. A branch scrapes the wall, fingernails on glass. Now curled in a corner, she lies asleep and dreaming.

Birds awake before the morning sun. She wonders where she is, remembers, falls asleep again. The birds are talking about her. An empty swallow's nest hangs above her head. Outside a dog barks. She can see two men through the window. They walk toward the house with guns. She flattens herself, along where floor meets wall. Her breathing is inside her. The dog circles the foot of her ladder, pawing and barking. The men talk beneath her. They laugh, shift their weight. She sees them on the other side, guns cocked and loaded.

Lunch Hour

THERE SHE is again. Can't she take her lunch hour somewhere else? Just because here there's a tree and a fountain . . . Why doesn't she go back to Utah? She thinks he's waiting for her. She's perfecting a letter to him. There she goes again! She must have six different versions by now. She's got them spread out on her knees: the one she typed at work, the one she scribbled yesterday, the one she wrote on the IRT subway. She's crossing things out; now she sits back and chews on her pen. Her lips are moving; she's smiling. She thinks Ralph is smiling too, she thinks she's writing phrases to make his heart leap inside him. She's actually giggling. She doesn't notice me staring at her blue eyes with too much mascara, her round girl's face and her foot, twitching like she's high on something. I undo the Saran Wrap from my bagel. The cream cheese sticks to my fingers. I take a large bite, chewing as I watch her. She's seeing him. He's at his mailbox: he rips open the letter before he reaches his door. She thinks he holds it to his chest before laying it near his bed; later when he can't sleep, he'll read it again. She doesn't know he stopped perusing them months ago; they're somewhere in his closet, in the box filled with loose papers, tax forms, and bills — he forgets which one.

Memorabilia

HE FOUND in a second-hand bookstore the book he'd given her. He'd written no message in it, yet he knew, as he turned it over in his hands, it had been his gift to her. If he'd written something — her name even — would she have kept it? Had she loved him so little? Or was it money that made her sell it? She couldn't have gotten very much for it though — was it meanness then? Indifference? He looked at the book more closely. A date was penciled in the corner: 6/86. She'd sold the book a year ago, a year and four months after they'd broken up, eight months after she'd last seen him. Why did he have to remember things? Dates, birthdays, conversations even — he could recall them exactly. He knew she did not remember these things, did not count the letters in a name, look at initials or birthdates as if they revealed some larger meaning than numbers, letters, names.

He bought the book. The saleswoman wrapped it in brown paper and it occurred to him to ask her, "Do you remember who sold the book to you?" She stared at him. "I haven't that kind of memory," was all she said.

I haven't that kind of memory, he repeated to himself as he walked into the street. But I have, he thought. He would have recalled her easily, would have been able to put a face to each book in the store. He knew this to be both a curse and a feat for him. It could please or embarrass him; he was forever recalling someone to his face who didn't remember him.

The sun felt strong as he walked down the street, brown package under his arm. Ah! There was the café they used to sit in, above it an apartment they'd once talked about owning. He hadn't gone into the café for over a year; now he walked right in. He found it changed: the walls had been painted an oily white where wallpaper had once been. But the place felt the same to him; its personality—the customers, the smoke-filled room, the smell of coffee—could not be painted over or changed. He chose a table they used to sit at.

He ordered coffee and undid the package. He flipped through the book; had she even read these pages? It smelled like the bookstore: old, .nusty. He remembered the last time he'd seen her. He'd been waiting for her, walking up and down a street near her own, knowing she'd be coming home from work soon. "What are you doing here?" she had asked, almost accused him. And he had told her that he took his laundry to the corner—it was the cheapest place around (did she believe him?). He walked her home and she declined to invite him inside (was she living with someone?). She had talked about her work; they'd said nothing personal, nothing about seeing each other. No, that wasn't right. He had told

her, "I'd like to invite you for a drink some evening." And she had screwed up her eyes and said,
"Maybe sometime . . ." He hadn't called or seen
her since then.

Did she still live there? Had she left the city,
her job? He supposed he could find out—he
drained his coffee, watched the words shift and
blur as he flipped through the pages of the book
he'd given her—

I trace a crack in the table
feel the wood, already separated
you watch my finger
tracing the route
you are planning
but there's a splinter you
don't see, I'll have
long after you've left me.

Letter to B.

LAST NIGHT I visited you again. There were lots of people, a sort of party going on. You looked like the man I'd seen on the L train, that is, the man who reminded me of you, except his hair was straighter, his sneakers newer. He sat down next to me, so close I could feel his arm through his jacket. I didn't want to look at him, looked at the window instead, but we were there: the unlikely couple, reflected in dirty glass.

I fought hard against jealousy as I saw you talking at length first to my sister, then to my best friend. I fought feeling that you should be more attentive to me—why should you, after all, except that I'd come all the way to visit you. At your invitation, I reminded myself. At last you spoke to me. "I want to show you something," you said. I followed you outside, out to a terraced garden. "Look," you said, "I have a Tree of Umbrellas." It was a grand tree, a magnificent tree, with umbrellas sprouting from each limb. "It belonged to my mother," you said. "It reminds me," I began— I wanted to impress you too—"of a garden I found in France . . ."

I have only one umbrella. On a different night I lost it—left it behind with a plant someone had given me as I ran to catch the E train. My plant, my umbrella: I struggle to recover them.

The Man I Want to Marry

I SAW the man I want to marry walking on the other side of the street—arms swinging, long strides—talking aloud to himself, noticing no one. People stepped aside as he walked by (he has that kind of presence) and he couldn't have been much older than 23 or 25, and the tail of his red shirt flapped after him.

Last night he was wearing his shirt the color of ripe tomato and I saw his hands: long fingers, nicotine-stained, broken nails, and his laugh was like a waterfall, tumbling down over rocks, boulders. I tumbled with him into a still dark pool, found his mouth underwater.

He showed me where he lives. It is dark like his mind; clothes are scattered like his thoughts, and the air smells of cigarettes, crusty socks, worn-out shoes. Here seasons are confused. We fall onto his bed and I feel his weight on top of me. His chin scrapes my cheeks; my face burns under his.

The clock stares at us from the side of the bed. Its face is broken. "I was going to change my life," the man I will marry says, "that's why I bought it. But it's so hard to remember to wind it, and I've already dropped it three times . . ."

The room seems to have lived through storms. Across the street the nightclub robs the dark with its bright lights and music, fluorescent green. Somewhere church bells chime the hour. I count eleven, twelve, thirteen — bury my face in his chest, my nose in his underarms. I taste onions: raw, bleeding. I trace the scars on his body — this one where he dove into a river and a tree trunk caught him. This one where he crashed his motorcycle. This one — when he was born.

Smell of salt sea: we are underwater. Here in the tangle of seaweed. Bubbles rise from his mouth. He is talking to me. Words I cannot see or hear. But he is talking. What he says escapes me. I strain to hear but all sound is enclosed, like the roar of an airplane, a sound you hear but that takes with it for a moment your ability to match sounds with words. A fish enters me. My body an ocean. Rippling. Water in my ears. I want all of him inside me. The ocean swallows an island, releases it once more.

Hollows of hunger. A place I hadn't known before. "These are places you must go," he tells me. It is dark and gnawing: a cave, hungry and black, to swallow us. Surely I will die here, or be left alone. He laughs. His laughter echoes in all of the rooms, takes me to a corner, a hard shell. I bump into walls, watch my body bruise. A pain: sharp through the roof of my mouth, through my abdomen, the sound teeth make when they grind . . . but it's gone. The room, black but soft, envelopes me: I am alone.

I saw him: arms swinging, long strides, shirt flapping behind him. He was singing as he walked. People stepped aside (he has that kind of presence) as I watched him walk away.

THERE WAS A WOMAN

There Was a Woman

THERE WAS a woman with a roomful of treasures who loved a certain man. And he loved her treasures. He would come into her house to see them. She had arranged them neatly: the box with buttons, green and gold, the one with miniature zebras, the pair of ivory feet. They invited his attention. For hours he would examine them, gently pulling up their lids, cautiously spilling out their contents. And the woman watched him. Delighted in his delight. She tempted him with her treasures, moving them to different rooms, placing her favorite — the horse that reared up onto its hindlegs — in the bedroom. So it was she caught him. Found it in herself to lock the house. Though she discovered, poor woman, that he was locked in his absorption. She would wind up the walking bear and wind up the horse, and he would follow their movements with his eyes, and she would follow his eyes with her own. Until his eyes watched so closely, she could no longer find them. She unlocked the house. She set him upon the dresser. "This one moves in perfect circles," she told the occasional visitor.

House of Gluttons

ONCE THERE was an innocent who visited a house of gluttons. He, shoeless and scared, asks for a bite to eat. They are laughing as they stuff themselves. Someone shows him in, sits him down. He stares, touching the place on his head where he has no hair. All around him are plates, clatter and chatter. He is handed a bone with meat. He holds it in his hand and watches. He wants to do it just right. He watches juice slobber down their chins, hears their raucous laughter, sees bits of food fly from their mouths. He brings the meat to his mouth. The meat is like the side of a cow to him. He bites but cannot chew. Someone is watching him. For a moment they stop laughing. They see how slowly he eats, how delicate his bites are. They are pointing at him and laughing again. They laugh so hard they forget to eat. "Eat this," they tell him, flinging him bread and pouring him wine. "Drink this!" Cups and plates are broken, the tablecloth is hurled, and the table upturned. He touches his head. His hair is wet from wine and the juice of meat. Holding his hands to his head, he stumbles from the house.

After He Moved

IT ARRIVED shortly after he moved out — moved in with another woman, younger than he or she — late in the day it came, just as dusk was falling. She thought at first she was imagining it, asked her children to have a look. Yes, they confirmed for her, it was there again, as it had been yesterday, preening its snow-white feathers carefully. She asked herself why it had chosen *her* roof (why not his?), why it came every evening without fail — what could it have in mind? She willed it away, assured herself as she woke: Today it will be gone . . . only to find it later on: too clean and white, too unusual for the area. She gathered her children around her, "It's an evil omen," she told them, twisting her fingers together, her forehead wrinkling as she said it. The older ones stared at her, "How can you be sure? It's white, after all," but the youngest had already collected stones, piled them high. Too small to reach very far; "I'll help you with that," his mother said, her aim growing sharper with each try.

4 of Us

THERE ARE four of us: the leader, a young woman, myself, and a wiry old man. "One of you must volunteer a dream," the leader says. It's the first time we've met; I'm reluctant to volunteer mine. "It's best if it's a recent one," the leader adds. "I have one," the old man says. "I first dreamt it when I was in college, but it's recurring." I think he must be seventy now. "I was in a classroom, I always sat toward the back . . ." The leader interrupts him, "Use the present tense; we must hear it described in the present." The old man coughs into a handkerchief. "Very well," he says. "I'm in a classroom. The professor is standing behind his desk. There's a window to his right. He raps his pen on the table 'Carl,' he says — Carl, that's me" the old man adds, "'Carl, have you got the answer?' I don't have the answer. I try to think of it nonetheless. The professor is waiting. I look at the window a moment and suddenly it comes to me and I raise my hand, 'I've got it! I've got it!' but he doesn't see me; he's calling on someone else now. And the thing is, that's how it always was: just when I had the answer . . . Not too long ago I was at a party and I saw him, you know this was years later, and I asked him, 'Why is it that just when I thought of the answer, you . . .'" The leader interrupts him. "Someone else?" he asks. "Remember, it's best if it's a recent one."

The Right Move

SHE HELD the washcloth to her cheek and searched her reflection. Found her eyes, staring blue, the freckles on her nose, and something that shouldn't have been there: a moustache of fine black hair. She couldn't stare it away.

She went to bed, hoping that sleep would erase it. She saw it as a shadow that chose to follow her, and like a dream, she had only to open her eyes to make it disappear.

In the morning she shuffled to the bathroom, blank and bleary-eyed, looking neither for the mirror nor the floor. She moved through the halls to white kitchen walls. Ate and dressed and went outside.

The day was like a myriad of others until she noticed her reflection in a car window; something dark claimed her upper lip. She hated the thought that anyone could see her, that many people had. She would go home. She would be seen nowhere.

She considered ways to be rid of it: razor blade, wart removal solution, chemicals for excess body hair. But she tried none of these. Given how it had visited her, how without past history it simply appeared, she felt she had no right to interfere. She hated her newly acquired hair, but judged it a matter for delicate decisions. With the right move it might leave her, for someone else perhaps — but what did she care?

She brought out the dark coat from her closet. She'd worn it once, after being woken by the sound of rain. But she'd hardly walked three blocks before she returned and closed the door. It made her look haggard, she thought, kept her hair out of place and her eyes forlorn.

She tried it on. She buttoned the three black buttons. Once they looked hideous and oversized. Now she liked them. They seemed to take charge.

She stood on street corners and at the fringe of crowds. She listened and nodded. She did not smile. She offered no information.

"Can you tell me how to get to State Street?"

"I don't know. I'm not from here."

An old man stopped her. "Right now I couldn't throw a stone ten yards. Used to be I could skin trees. I'd have five knives and five tries and I'd do it every time. I'd put a dime to the tree, see..."

"I have to go now."

She felt her strangeness was becoming familiar. She wanted to be alone. She rented an attic room, wrapped a scarf round her nose, seated herself with a view of down below. A branch hid her window, as if the tree had lent an arm to shield her from view. It was not a busy street. She saw a father and child, a boy kicking stones, four girls who laughed between sentences. They never looked up but kept their feet to the pavement and their hands in their jackets.

She gleaned nothing from their posture or smiles or snatches of talk that reached her. Once she thought she saw something remarkable, but it was only a pigeon, standing still and going nowhere. It had waddled to the edge of the square where it stood, scrawny and grey, a miniature scarecrow. When she looked again, it was gone.

Guessing Game

SHE ASKED me to guess her profession. She'd sat down next to me on the train, adjusting her large plastic bag so it rested at her ankles. Her hair fell in thick strands; her eyes were heavily made up, her skin wrinkled and aged. "Homeless person" was what came to mind, but I could never have said that to her. I tried to get past the word "homeless"; for some reason "salesclerk" was what found its way around the word. She laughed good-naturedly. "Salesclerk! Can you imagine me a salesgirl? That's wonderful, but no, honey, that's not me, guess again . . ." I studied her once more. Did she really work, wasn't she just pulling my leg? I felt myself sweating. "Schoolteacher?" I asked tentatively. She laughed again. "Schoolteacher! That's sweet, but no, not me . . . try again, honey . . ." What were those huge stains on her coat? And her hands were coarse, cracked and lined. What did she do? Wash someone's laundry? I felt my face redden under the strain, "I don't know," I stammered, "I really can't guess anymore . . ." "Can't you guess? Can't you try? Is it really so hard?" "No, I'm sorry," I said, aware of my own inadequacies at this strange game. But it was my stop—quickly I stood up, while someone else, armed with shopping bags, landed in the spot I'd vacated.

Liza Jane

HE MOVED north from the city, found a town, not too large or small, a town with wide streets and wide cars, without hills, without a view.

He chose an apartment, one of seven townhouses on Lincoln Street, between Ninth and Tenth. Once inside, he found little reason to go out. He pulled down the shades and bolted the door.

It bothered him that he could hear a child crying through the walls. Even worse, he thought, was the mother who cried back at the child. He hung rugs on the wall so as not to hear it, this screaming battle between mother and daughter, but they eased neither the sound nor his mind.

He felt hot during the night and cold during the day. He was plagued by a scene from the war. The scene was the jungle. A small girl traipsed through selling Coca-Cola. He had heard footsteps from behind and shot at her. He'd tried to cry as he told his wife this scene from the war. But he felt nothing as he watched the tears well in her eyes. And knew he had to leave her.

He had chosen this town, full of shades of white and grey, hoping to live out the blandness inside him. Not to betray the living. Emotions. He had none.

He had heard that the end was near. He wondered how best to prepare. He thought he was readier than most, with no communication from the outside. His wife had failed to track him down, or perhaps she hadn't tried. He thought of her at times, remembering that he'd loved her. She was Esther and he had been Alan. But that was before. Now she only frightened him, like the woman next door, with her screaming and crying. And always it seemed directed at him, because he didn't try to protest or assist her, but felt the blankness surface, his face like white paper.

Perhaps this woman next door was the woman his wife. They seemed to share the same frenzy, forever spilling anguish and anger into the air. Then he would not give into her strange form of torture, he decided. But realized he had still one emotion lingering within him: fear.

And it was fear, this emotion that seemed to tangle from the inside and wrap itself around him, that he was most afraid of.

He let himself open one of the blinds, perhaps looking for an escape route for his fear. The next townhouse was shared by three girls. He could see them through their window. They did not have blinds. Perhaps they were college girls. He noticed during the day they were gone.

One day he saw a man knock on the girls' door. The girls weren't home. The man knocked for a long time before realizing. Alan watched him scribble a note on a piece of paper, fold it, then pin it to the door. But the wind was strong and the note looked like it would soon blow away.

Alan ran to the door. He forgot he had to un-bolt it. He struggled with the metal knobs, finally jerked it open. The man was past the third town-house, walking.

"The wind will blow it away!" Alan shouted after him. "It will blow away . . . The note! They won't find it . . ." The man had walked farther away. He hadn't turned his head. He hadn't heard anything. Other people on Lincoln Street were staring.

Alan looked at them, realizing. A violent shiver ran down his spine. He went to the girls' door, removed the note carefully. He saw the man had used only a crack on the door to hold it there; he hadn't even used a pin.

He didn't read it. Only the outside: Liza Jane. Inside his house, he shivered again. He had the note in his hands. He dropped it quickly on the table, a bomb made of paper. How was he to de-liver it to them? He would have to explain. He didn't want to talk to them. They were young and always laughing; who knew what they were thinking? Easier to slip it under their door. He took the note and went again to their door.

In his house he felt better. People, it seemed, could no longer recognize common perils. It was quiet in the room. He stood still, listening. The baby was preparing to cry. The sound, he had learned, which was no sound at all, forecast the storm. A wave of cold washed over him. He was trapped by the wife-woman and her child in a house that was supposed to free him.

And then suddenly it occurred to him: the girls would never see the note at all. Didn't they have carpet on the floor? He rushed to the open blind. Yes, he thought he could see a bluish green carpet on the floor. Then he had slipped the note under the carpet! For that reason the man had put it on the door . . . Oh, if only he'd realized!

Now he would have to tell them, when they came home. How he dreaded that. To knock on the door, as the man had, to say the words: "There's a note under your carpet . . ." He would have to explain. Was it best to leave the incident alone? He wondered. But perhaps the note was important, crucial even. Oh, if only he'd read it, just to know . . . But he'd seen only "Liza Jane" and what could that mean?

He paced the room uneasily. He felt he was both sweating and shivering. Soon they'd be coming home. What time was it? But he kept no clock in the room. It seemed they arrived just after dark. Perhaps another hour or so. He sat at his table and stared through the open blind. The mother was screaming at her child. She wouldn't stand for no.

"SHUT UP! Take your bottle! Take it!"

He bit down on his thumbnail. No, don't do it again, he prayed

"I said take the goddam bottle!"

He heard the bottle crash against the floor. He

went to the wall, "Stop it, please stop it!" he pleaded. The rugs muffled his cry. He pounded on them. His fist made soft thuds. The baby broke into a new wave of crying, drowning his own.

Beauty Contest

HE PASSED me as I walked my route to work. An old man, I wouldn't have noticed him except that his faded blue eyes locked with mine as we crossed paths. "You'll never win a beauty contest. I *hate*—women," he said with contempt. I stared at him. What had he said, what kind of women? I wanted to ask him, but why give him that satisfaction? Besides, I was angry, "You'd never win one either," I wanted to add, though he was long since past. My eyes smarted, I felt my face stiffen. How dare he make commentary on the women he passed? I saw his pallid face, his mouth etched with scorn, as I turned the sound over in my mind, racked my aural memory. . . grave, it had sounded like "grave," but "grave women"—it made no sense. Heavy women, maybe? Or, strong women? Was it what I was wearing—I was dressed all in black—women who wear black—no, he hadn't said that. I chose to forget it, but it came back to me at odd times during the day—catching a glimpse of myself in a store window as I walked past—and later in the week, when my mind should have been on the report I was writing I tried still to decipher the old man's remark. And then I forgot. It was buried. Until yesterday, coming home by the same route, I noticed an old man, slightly stooped, unremarkable except that he was staring at me intently. Just as I recognized him as the same man, his eyes locked with mine, "A beauty," he said, as if he'd just stabbed a prize.

Matchstick Woman

THE WOMAN reminded her of a matchstick: a matchstick with its head burnt but not yet fallen off, still hanging on. What a terrible thought. But the woman unnerved her. She was always popping up unexpectedly, her spiky hair and ragged clothes taking Julie by surprise. She was so thin, with legs like brittle twigs and a laugh that seemed to come from nowhere. It seemed to Julie that the matchstick woman was mocking her, that her obscene laughter was meant for her—a ridiculous notion—there was nothing odd or laughable about her, but why was the woman always crossing her path like a black cat, an ill omen?

The other day she'd gone to pick up her clothes at the dry cleaners. She was about to pay when she heard a thin squeaky voice, a voice that seemed to walk tall stilts down narrow hallways: "Good afternoon." The man behind the counter answered civilly, "Good afternoon." Julie had not looked up (she was counting out change) and heard the squeaky voice so close to her that a shiver ran down her spine: "A truck almost ran me over last night."

It was the matchstick woman, standing so close Julie could see her skin, smudged brown, the glint of craziness in her dark eyes. For a moment those eyes held her; quickly she paid the clerk and hurried out the store.

She kept looking back over her shoulder as she walked home and once, in doing so, she bumped into an older man, had to apologize effusively. But the woman was not following her; Julie couldn't see her anywhere. How soundless she was—the way she'd stolen up on her, the way she'd just disappeared. Julie shook her head as if to shake off the woman, the sensation she'd left her with.

"A truck almost ran me over last night . . ." She shivered. Had it really happened or did the woman only imagine catastrophes? But maybe she really did get run over once, that would explain her wackiness, and Julie thought yes, it happened once, some years ago, and she's never been the same since. She fumbled for the keys to her apartment, found them and suddenly realized she'd left her clothes at the dry cleaners.

Goddam that creepy lady, she said to herself as she retraced her steps. If she hadn't sneaked up behind her with that weird story . . . Because she would be late for work now, and yesterday she'd arrived late as well, though that had been no one's fault but her own . . .

She retrieved her clothes from the smiling clerk (did he enjoy other people's forgetfulness?) and she thought to mention, "That sure was a strange lady who came in here, I don't know about her . . ." The man continued smiling, but raised his eyebrows as if to ask: who? "That woman who was just in here with that teeny voice — " And now he knitted his eyebrows, frowned. "Who said she got run over by a truck . . ." And still he looked confused, couldn't recall her. "Oh never mind." She picked up her clothes and left the store.

So he hadn't thought her strange — well what did that say about him? I won't think about her anymore, she thought, I'm going to forget her just as he did — oh to have a mind like a sales-clerk, to think of nothing but payments and debts — what else? But surely their minds were no different? So why hadn't he remembered her? But I'm not going to think of it, she reminded herself.

She changed quickly, changed again and changed once more because nothing seemed to look right on her. So why do I look fat in this dress if I've lost so much weight? she thought, convinced herself she didn't really — there was no time to contemplate it further — and left her apartment for the nearest subway station.

In the tunnel she saw the woman again; she seemed to be walking the length of the passage toward her, grinning widely. Julie averted her eyes as she walked past her, heard: "Just now a dog almost bit me," and then couldn't help her-self; she looked at the woman whose dark eyes widened while her voice continued, a thin squeak, "A big dog, a ferocious dog, he almost bit me . . ."

Julie kept on walking. On the train she straightened her dress, ran her fingers through her hair. For a moment she closed her eyes but the voice greeted her from the black: "He almost bit me." She looked around at the other passengers. No one was staring at her. No one seemed to have noticed her. She took a book from her bag; she would read it for the next six stops, until her own appeared.

Rabid, rabid, rabid. There seemed to be no other words printed on the page in her book: the woman is rabid. Infected. Don't you dare come near me, she thought. I can't help you, can't do anything. Just keep away—please. Keep away from me.

She realized she was mouthing the words, saying them half-aloud, but how else would they have any effect, any power? But they'd receded now—the woman, the words—it was her stop next. She closed her book, filed off with the other passengers.

She did not run into the woman again that week and there were other things—her job, the fact that George had not called—to keep her mind occupied. And why hadn't George called? He got mad at things, small things, and took it out on her. He was so touchy, was easily hurt, but why should she be punished for it?

She saw him on Saturday. It was a warm day, bright, and George was in a good mood; she loved him then. They walked arm in arm, stopping to look in store windows at things they could never afford to buy. George mentioned an antique statue, something he'd had his eye on. Did she want him to show her? Of course she did, most of all to see what kind of statue would fascinate him—she couldn't imagine. The store was closed. They stood, straining to see through the glass, the dark of the store.

"I can't see it—do you think they would have sold it already?" George asked, his hands shielding his eyes, now pressed against the glass. And then she caught her reflection: spiky hair, eyes shining black. She looked behind her but she couldn't find the matchstick woman anywhere. She touched her face, her hair.

"C'mon, let's go," George said. Still she ran her fingers through her hair, touched her lips, her nose.

"Julie, you seem nervous," George was saying to her.

"Yes," she said and her voice sounded strange to her, too high, "Last night I almost got stuck in an elevator . . ."

"You did? Why didn't you tell me?"

"I don't know . . ." she said, seeing herself suddenly locked in the small box, pressing buttons, ramming herself against the door, and wondered why it had only just occurred to her.

His Name Was Not Sam

HE HATED how she went on like that. How could anyone have so much talking? Where did it all come from? Bubbling like a spring, gurgling up out of black . . . No, he wasn't listening; just these sounds he heard—some cooing and trilling. He looked at her now, sitting, eyes bright, and her voice . . . He turned away.

He used to answer her. Had told her of himself, pieces of his life. Then realized that the telling (his talking) sparked more of her own. He hadn't even finished and she was nodding her head, eyes even brighter; it all reminded her of something she had seen, somewhere she'd been, things which had happened.

He had hoped his silence would be enough for both of them. He clothed all his words, hid them back inside. Felt them in the lining of his suit jacket. Then heard his mind thinking, thought he was hungry. He walked into the kitchen seeing potatoes, sliced and fried. But when he looked, he couldn't find any.

Do we have potatoes? he asked and searching still, he found her at his arm, saying we should have some in the drawer, here but did you look? Here, in this bag, oh but these are soft, going bad, but we could get some new ones, sweet ones, with red skins—have you tried? Good fried, but oh, even nicer baked — not too much — with some butter, the real kind . . .

Things were muddled now. He didn't think he wanted them after all.

But what do you mean? You surely do if you said so, and the store's not faraway, open still, almost next door, and with such a nice man — the one who's cashier. But be sure to get the red ones . . .

There was money in his fist. He was being nudged out the door. People filled the street and walked on by. He stood for a moment, dizzied by the night air. He walked, hands in pockets, thinking something had gone wrong. He had been quiet, safe inside, and now here he was on the street wondering why he had come, where he should turn (he passed the grocery now on his left) and this man was calling him Sam, hey, how ya doin Sam, where ya been, it's good to see ya Sam, I say, I always feel good when I see ya Sam, I always have a good day (and now he called after him), bye Sam! We'll see ya later! So long Sam!

His name was not Sam. Crazy people — how they cluttered his mind. He walked, shoes slapping the pavement, to hear himself think. Think of what to do now. He felt hungry. He would walk into the next café he saw. He would order French fries.

He ate them plain. He didn't want salt and he didn't want ketchup. He ate them from the wax paper in the red basket, one by one. He didn't pause as he ate them, tasting duller each time. Once he felt he might not finish, seeing how they still piled high. He ate with both hands, chewing faster now. And then his hand touched the paper, where the grease stained it clear. He didn't mind the sea of talk around him. He closed his eyes and felt himself alone with the ocean at his ears, rushing then flowing. It calmed him with no particular words to hear, and his mind washed clean by the sound.

The voice rose up when he opened the door. What made you so late? Did you find them? Did he talk to you—the cashier, the one with the long beard, a friendly sort, don't you think? But you didn't get them, did you? Was it closed? Where did you go? And the money—did you spend that too? He closed his eyes not to hear.

He lay in bed feeling the apartment like a shell around him. Noise banged from outside as cars streamed by. The glass shivered.

During the day he walked the apartment. Avoided the kitchen. If he went near he was sure to hear the voice. It was coming from there now, almost stuttering—why? Not streaming, but sputtering. Then silences, then thrusts of words. He closed himself in a room, listened to the cars rattle the window. The screeching and starting, the speeding and stopping. Then the banging at the door, the rattling of the room. The hollow shell reverberating. Until closing his eyes, he heard the voice at his ears.

He went to the window, opened it wide. He eased himself onto the windowsill, jumped to the pavement outside. He looked straight ahead, his feet stepping faster now, hearing, hey Sam! How ya doing? Come over and talk to me Sam . . .

He heard the voice from behind; it was trailing him. Now at his heels, at his neck, inside his ears . . . He ran. And running, tried to shake it off, like a flame that had caught his jacket, set him on fire, spreading as he ran.

In His Absence

SHE FOUND one morning, under the last sip of tea, at the bottom of the cup, a circle of roses staring up at her. How was it she had never seen them? She went through the cupboard, pulled out all the plates and bowls. They were there — patterned on the rims of china.

"The things I am discovering . . ." she wrote. "How is it I never noticed the painted roses on the china cups? Had you seen them and never showed me?" Then she described them in detail — how a thin stroke of paint could create such a blossom. Because if one looked long enough, that's all it was — a brush stroke of paint, a swirl of color, nothing more . . . Yet they blossomed before her.

She wrote him this and more. She sealed the letter in an envelope, addressed it overseas. She had the letter weighed and sent. He knew her now, the clerk, had often handed her the crisp blue envelopes. There had been so many at first, sometimes two in one day, often six in one week. But they had slowed. Now there might be one.

But the clerk had nothing for her. Walking home she saw what she hadn't noticed before. Near her house grew a pear tree. Its branches bowed down under the weight of its fruit — bronze and thick-skinned. They were hard like

103

rocks, but shapelier, though rather squat for pears.

"How is it I never saw the pears? Did you know and never show me?" She told him how in the dark she heard them fall, how she woke to find more nestled in the grass. "I've lined them on my windowsill, though I don't think I shall eat them, while they sit so squat and firm."

A ROBBER IN
THE HOUSE

Weekdays

MONDAY, TUESDAY, Wednesday, Thursday, and Friday she forgot about the plant. It sat on its stand in the corner of the room with its healthy green leaves, its commendable height. The curtain drooped from its rod. The bookcase tilted to one side. The plant sat there, firm in its soil.

Saturday he rose from bed (she watched him), lifted the plant from its stand, placed it in the sink with water to spray over it. He spent the morning in the bathroom while she lay in bed, finding patterns in the cracks in the ceiling. When at last she rose, she found it in the kitchen, filling the sink with its leafiness. She felt the need to do the dishes, to rinse out the milk bottle. She wanted to fill the kettle with water. It was in the way. She didn't want to touch it, wanted him to lift it out. She waited. Waited until he emerged from the bathroom, dressed, moved about the kitchen, telephoned (she watched him), picked up crusts of bread and ate them. She felt she must remind him, "Could you take the plant out of the sink?" Yes, he said he would.

At night he took it to her corner of the room, its soil dark and moist. She faced the tilting bookcase, the drooping curtain. For a week she didn't see it. Saturday it was in the sink again. It seemed to have grown. Its leaves reached the cupboard's base, then bent and splayed. When she walked past the sink, its leaves brushed her skin.

She lay on the bed, seeing the cracks in the ceiling like the plant's splayed leaves. Another week and it had grown too large for the sink. He placed it in the bathtub with water to spray over it. She sensed it growing in the tub, basking behind the shower curtain.

The bookcase toppled over. The curtains slid from their rods. Cracks in the ceiling split deeper. When it rained, water dripped through. The house was growing, tilting, cracking.

She felt the plant all around her. Its branches reached out like fans. Its topmost leaves formed a canopy. He no longer moved it. It was watered by the rain.

Shoes

SHE WAS a big woman who'd gotten larger instead of smaller since they'd married, her beauty more and more lost in her round pumpkin face, her eyes sunken like seeds. Still, he had hopes for her, if only she'd pull herself together, take more pains with her appearance. He himself was preoccupied with it, often spending money on small gifts for her: earrings, a new sweater, a colored band for her hair.

There was a small shoe shop down the road from where they lived and he often found himself going in there. He liked the arrangement of the store: carpeted and with a plush sofa on which to sit and try on shoes, and then handbags, jewelry, trinkets set in among the shoes. The saleswoman was extremely helpful. She suggested several styles to compliment a heavy-set woman, with one pair in particular promising to flatter her. There was a choice of black or red; he chose red, paid the young woman, thanking her profusely while she wrapped the shoes in tissue paper, as carefully as two eggs nestled in cardboard.

He held out the package to his wife. She undid the paper not so much carefully as cautiously, as if whatever he'd bought might explode with shaking. In fact their color, a deep lipstick red, seemed to burst from the package.

"The color is all wrong," was what she said.

"Honey, please, try them on."

She obliged him, but he could see she didn't care for them, seemed more annoyed than pleased at the trouble he'd taken to choose them.

"We'll take them back. You can exchange them . . ."

She nodded, thrusting them into their tissue paper and box.

The saleswoman was as usual extremely helpful. But his wife merely nodded her answers, offering nothing of herself, silent and unmoved by the saleswoman's and his compliments. And then it happened, what mortified him even now to remember: his wife punched her. He sometimes doubted it had happened, yet he could see it still: his wife putting her coat back on, the young woman bustling by, two pairs of shoes in her hands, his wife's fist shooting through her sleeve to hit her on her shoulder as she walked past.

"Oh I'm so sorry," his wife said. "Did I hurt you?"

"No, it's nothing, nothing at all," the woman replied, but he could see the hurt and surprise in her blue green eyes, and he longed to stay and comfort her, to wrap her in his arms and carry her somewhere, lie beside her; he felt fragile and full of love for her.

Watch

IF HE knew he would not love her. If he knew. He would not love her if he knew. Like now: how she is lying in bed, naked, a candle by the bedside. She studies her underarm hair. She pulls out a strand, places it near the flame and watches it curl up into itself. An acrid smell. If he knew this about her. She plucks out another one, listens to it sizzle. The last time she saw him they talked over pizza in a restaurant. He cut his with a knife and fork. In between bites he used his napkin. She noticed his watch then: a thick gold band, a square clock face. Not so large as to be ostentatious, but it looked expensive. She remembered his voice on the phone, "Why? What time is it?" He had called her at three. She'd waited all day for his call; she'd given up thinking he would. "Why? What time is it?" when all along he knew. He had a watch that would always be accurate. Her own watch had two faces, one set above the other one. Two small faces set vertically. He had asked her the meaning of it. She shrugged. "It was a gift. Fashion, I guess." He stared at it. "It's eerie," he said. Eerie? She hadn't seen it that way. Humorous, maybe. "It's really very eerie," he said, finally looking away from it. She watches the flame of her candle. At any moment the phone might ring.

Gunshot

SHE IMAGINED shooting him. One shot through the back of his head, right beneath his bald spot. Blood spattered on the carpet, formed a sticky mass, round and red. Or she'd send a bullet through the mail. He'd open the white envelope to find a single bullet nestled in the empty pocket. The one meant for his head. Or she'd leave a message on his machine: the sound of a gun going off. He'd come home to his one-room apartment, see the blinking red light, switch on the machine before he turned on the lights. And then he'd hear it: a gunshot ripping through the dark of his apartment. The bullet meant for his head. She felt sure he'd get the message.

Closer

SHE HAD woken one night for no apparent reason: no sound, no light outside or in the room. She felt only darkness around her, and one small question, growing larger and louder: what made her love him?

During the day it was all so clear. She could see him with his clean white teeth, his thick brown hair. She sensed his height, a height she had to look up to. And his mind: filled with books she hadn't read, authors she'd never heard of. He spoke in earnest of these things and she listened quietly, glad to watch his lips move, his teeth shine, glad to look into his eyes. She saw him when he wasn't there in the photograph beside her.

That he was extraordinary, she was sure. For one thing, he was a writer. Often he would break off an engagement to spend time before the typewriter. This she understood. It was a long and tedious process with not much hope for results. So she didn't ask to see any—results, that is. He detailed his plots for her, long and elaborate they were, and she sensed a mind that was leagues away from her. Though distance didn't perturb her. She saw herself as a buoy near the shore, something he could bump into and grasp onto. And from his clutch and grasp, she'd drift farther from the shore. Drifting didn't disturb her. She only hoped she'd journey closer, past the edges of his mind, to the heart of his genius.

Now she wondered. Wanted to be sure this man was a genius. Then cursed herself for wondering. Yet doubt trickled in, like signals from the shore. Certain visions came and stood before her — of him, his clothing for instance. It was ordinary, and yet its very plainness disturbed her. She looked for some sign — a red scarf, a checkered tie — something to distinguish him from the other grey-suited men she knew and had seen. But he wore nothing she could seize upon, though he changed his clothes regularly, and owned suits of varying shades of grey and grey brown, and shirts which varied from white to light blue.

She saw his house. It was neat, reflecting a certain order; this was true. Yet somehow she'd expected disarray, a labyrinth of mess and clutter as complex as the mind that created its design. She'd thought books would line each and every wall: too many for the shelves, she'd find them on the floor, in corners, stacked in boxes. But there weren't many, and these in the bedroom, out of view. Nor was there anything to hint at the foreign lands he'd seen (and these he had described) — no odd trinket to evoke any other time or place than the one they stood in. She saw: a new house complete with garage, and a backyard that didn't extend far. Inside there was yellow shag carpet, lamps to match, and furniture placed in the corners of the rooms. Nothing on the wall but a calendar: this was Tuesday, October 18. Only the typewriter relieved her—on a clean desk with a stack of fresh paper to one side. But why was so little on the walls? It frightened her almost. It seemed worse than ordinary; it seemed very, very bare.

Now as she looked to the ceiling of her dark room, she accepted these traits as further proof of his genius. Just as his clothing disguised his exceptional mind, so did his house. They seemed to evidence a great need to appear ordinary. Dressed in his grey suits and white shirts, he would never be thought otherwise.

She looked for further signs of his obsession. She remembered that he ate only plain food. He liked his steak medium-rare, and this with just a touch of salt and pepper. He didn't ask for ketchup with his eggs. In restaurants he never ordered the dishes with foreign names, but stuck (obstinately, it seemed) to the American dinners. Once, when trying to choose from a large selection of omelets, he'd asked her what scallions were, and she, baffled by his apparent ignorance, took some moments to reply. Now, on reflection, she judged the question in keeping with the man. Besides, scallions were but a small detail and details only clutter great minds.

So she ignored the question that had woken her, thinking she had solved it, thinking it would

115

go away of its own accord. Yet doubt persisted, like the occasional twitch in her left eye, it refused to be ignored. But no (after she'd turned onto her side, her back, her stomach, trying again and again to turn away from the question), he could be nothing but extraordinary.

She continued to see him, meeting him for lunch or dinner, or sometimes breakfast, listened to his latest plot (he was by now, far into a novel), smiled (though somewhat slower) as she looked into his eyes. She wondered if she were journeying farther from the ordinary and closer to the truly extraordinary. She seemed to be drifting. Yes, she thought she must be.

His Wife

HE HAD a wife that was always getting lost. How this could be so, he hadn't the least idea. If she'd never driven the roads before, he'd understand . . . but she got lost on roads she'd been driving for months now. She explained it this way: I was upset by a certain student in class, my mind was on that and not on the road, I was upset that I hadn't taught well. Besides, it was foggy and dark. But other times her teaching had gone exceptionally well and she still missed her turn, drove for hours on back roads trying to find her way back. He wondered if she didn't do it purposely so he'd lie awake worrying about her, and here the weather seemed to conspire with her—against him—it rained every Monday evening when she taught her class and once it had even snowed, a full month out of season.

He didn't like the impression it left him with, the obvious one: that his wife wasn't too sharp, not smart enough to remember her turns, despite the rain and dark, and then the other one, creeping up behind the first but still in shadow, not yet clearly seen or felt: that in the middle of the night she was journeying past marshes and bogs, through twisted tangled tree vines, wisps of fog, swerving to avoid the night animals, raccoons and deer, eyes shining unnaturally, like those

caught by flashbulbs in a photograph; driving
down road after road after road without him.

Onion

THE MOST typical of foods affected him strangely. Not at first but afterward, gradually over time, it was onions most of all that made his head pound and his stomach turn. She no longer cooked with them, did not make the onion pie she'd learned in France, *tarte des oignons*, that her own family had asked for again and again. She learned to substitute garlic for taste; for crunch she chose celery and in general made do with other spices, roots, and vegetables and did not think she missed them at all.

Only once in a supermarket without him she chose one for her cart, forgetting or putting aside for a moment his violent reaction to them.

She peeled it for soup, placed it on the cutting board to chop into slices.

"What are you doing?" Her husband stood in the doorway. "What are you going to do with that?"

"What?" she said, looking down at the clear white shape on the wooden cutting board, as if seeing its unmistakable onionness for the first time. "I don't know . . ." she said. "I'm putting it back." He watched her take it to the refrigerator where she placed it in the vegetable drawer, toward the back. Only on certain days does she notice it, lost as it is in the refrigerator's whiteness.

Knee-Deep

IT HAD occurred to her that there was another life running along beside hers, a stream she'd walked along, crossed even, but never entered, never sank up to her knees in, never swam in. It was not a mistake to realize this, but to follow it, to leave her clothes on the bank and enter the stream — perhaps this was not what she should have done. But then, these and other considerations had to be left behind like her clothes, her outer wrappings.

She'd left them all behind, had divorced her husband (it still amazed her how quickly that final arrangement had been made), had moved to another part of town. She saw some of her former friends and these told her she was changed, given easily to distraction, but how to explain —? She had a lover, one she saw infrequently, who sometimes disappeared for days, but she was sure she loved him more deeply than she'd ever loved her husband. It's true she saw him only now and then, but she felt the relationship to be nevertheless demanding. Once she dreamed that he was leaning on her, his chest against her back, a weight she was almost carrying as she walked into her room. "I don't like this room," he told her as they entered, and her husband, who had been sitting in a corner, fiddling with something or other, looked up to ask him, "Then what are you doing here?" Well, that was very like her husband, she had rationalized: trying to possess her still, to arrange her life for her. Though perhaps he had only her own good in mind? Well, it wasn't her own good she was after, but this other life she felt compelled to put her foot in, to stand knee-deep in.

Her lover was nothing like her husband. Or perhaps they weren't so different after all — ? Because he would also say: this or that is good for you. Was it only their idea of good that differed? Because once she'd locked herself out of her apartment. Recently moved, she hadn't yet made another set of keys; not even her lover had one. And she couldn't get a locksmith; it was past seven and all shops were closed. She'd gone to her lover's apartment only to find he wasn't home. (Where was he? Where did he go when he wasn't with her?) Panic struck her then because what other option was open to her? She was too embarrassed to call her husband; pride kept her from calling friends. But where could she go? Surely her lover would be home soon . . .

She'd wandered the streets in the darkening city. A car stopped, some men invited her inside. She hurried away from them. A beggar woman greeted her, armed with her children. "Can't you see I'm as poor as you?" she felt like asking, though she knew it wasn't true, was a state of mind only: without a home to go to, with only fifty cents in her pocket (she'd left her apartment to buy a newspaper), and for a moment she wished she could ask the woman for a square of her cardboard, just to have a place to sit, her own part of the sidewalk . . . but she only shrugged the woman away.

It was getting darker. She felt the city was somehow forbidden to her, a woman alone, without a car, with no money on her. Even the restaurants, the cafés she'd sit alone in during the day, said to her she couldn't enter. Parks and narrow streets that normally invited her looked dark and sinister, and the brightly lit windows of apartments seemed to mock her. She walked faster. She no longer knew where she was walking; her feet took her and her eyes didn't wander but looked straight in front of her. Somehow she'd made it to where her lover lived, and yes he was home, and she'd spent the night with him. But he hadn't sympathized as she'd imagined he would, had only said: It's good for you to feel homeless for a change, you shouldn't eat for a few days to know hunger too. It's good for you . . .

Oh, he resented her for her money. But didn't she work for it (and it wasn't so much after all) and wasn't she always lending him some? He did not work, though he had before she met him. He lived in a one-room apartment with everything he needed scattered on the floor. What he needed wasn't very much: three shirts, two pairs of pants, socks, shoes, some books, cigarettes . . . He was always saying: This way I can pick up and go whenever I want to, there's nothing to stop me, I can take everything with me, which always made her vaguely uneasy. If he would not let possessions hold him back, he would not let people hold onto him . . . But this had been their understanding from the beginning: they were lovers, not possessors of one another.

He'd criticized the sheer amount of her possessions and she'd agreed with him to some extent, enough to sell most of her furniture, much of her clothes and half of her book collection. Of the books she'd kept, most were scattered in his room; she'd lent them to him.

She'd missed her books though and wandered one day into a second-hand bookstore, thinking she would buy some more. She was browsing through *Le Morte d'Arthur*, when some commotion in the back room made her look up. She saw a man in a long rumpled overcoat through the open door, another overcoated man with him. She watched them. It was like watching a play; the man was acting. She realized he was selling used books, being dramatic about it, bargaining for better prices while he gesticulated wildly. His friend and the bookstore manager — his audience — were laughing. And suddenly she realized that this man, so frenzied and dramatic, was her lover. It was him and yet it wasn't, not the man she knew, because she had never seen the overcoat, the look in her lover's eyes. She stepped forward to greet him and then stopped. They were her books he was selling.

She wanted to run up, to grab the stack of books off the table, to look in his eyes, ask him: "Why are you doing this to me?" But something held her, silenced her, and she retreated into a dark corner of the store, leafing nervously through books as she watched him. He looked triumphant in his long overcoat as he strode to the cash register with his friend. He didn't see her. And she saw his friend: a tiny moustache, green eyes, he seemed the color of grey green to her and he looked both young and old and she didn't trust him. They strode out the door, a pair of—what? Conspirators? She emerged from her dark corner. She'd only wanted to see which direction they'd go but she found herself following them.

Laughter sprinkled their conversation, but she wasn't near enough to hear their words. And then she saw them link arms and do a little dance, laugh, keep on walking, their arms linked together. Her eyes smarted; she felt dizzy, but still she kept after them. It seemed to her that if her lover turned now, if his eyes happened on her, he wouldn't recognize her, wouldn't see her. She felt she had entered a part of his world she was not meant to, that in this world there was no place for her, that she was in fact, invisible.

She wished she could turn around, go home, but something made her continue after him, just as something held her back in the store. They went into a shop to buy beer; they stood in the street drinking it in quick gulps.

And then he turned and saw her, called out to her, friendly but too loud, "Hey! What are you doing here?" So he could see her after all, yet she imagined herself a phantom, white, all color drained from her face, and now she felt too guilty of following him, of spying, to accuse him: You sold my books. She bit back the words, oh but they tasted bitter inside, words she should have uttered, not kept to herself, but it made no sense to accuse him now, on the street, away from the scene of the crime . . . He was introducing her to his friend; it seemed his name was Lester, and Lester was smiling widely, a smile that seemed sincere. This confused her; hadn't he recognized his enemy, his rival? She tried to smile back at him, this grey green person, this part of her lover she had just discovered. And realized then he would not hate her, would not feel the jealousy she felt of him; he knew his place in her lover's life was large, what was left to her was a small corner only. She remembered all the times she'd gone to her lover's and he hadn't been there, the nights he was neither at his place nor hers . . .

We are lovers, not possessors of one another . . . The words stumbled together in her mind, and behind them, cutting a clearer trail: but you've betrayed me.

She realized they were shifting uneasily before

125

her, waiting. She was supposed to say or do something to relieve them of this weighty silence. Why should she do that for them, give them that gift? But she did: "I must be going now," and they quickened their smiles. "Nice meeting you," Lester offered, and from her lover: a light kiss and "I'll be by tonight."

She suffered his touch and turned her back on them. She couldn't feel her legs as they took her away, only a great pressure at her back (their eyes?). She walked the street she'd often walked home yet everything looked different to her: a paled sky, the air whitened, as if it were hiding something, and she saw in the men and women who passed her that their eyes were veiled also; even the small child standing in a doorway looked up at her with eyes that didn't see her. For a moment the street was silent. She heard no voices or laughter; she felt only a thick mist descending, enveloping her.

But she couldn't stay here. Now she must find her way back to that other world, that one she knew better, because tonight her lover would deny Lester, would tell her he loved her, and the books, already stacked on the store shelves, would never be mentioned.

A Robber in the House

SHE LIES facing him. He is thin, dark-haired, older than she is by twelve years. And he loves her. She wonders why she lets him. Tomorrow she'll tell him. "We can't see each other anymore. You're going to suffer; I see it in your eyes. I won't let you, won't be responsible for your future."

He lies facing her. She is pale with blue green eyes and younger than he is by several years. He doesn't know how many, has never asked her. It makes no difference to him. He watches her and wonders how to keep her from leaving him.

They lie facing one another and hear a key turn in the door, the steps of someone in the living room.

My roommate, she thinks.

"A robber," he says.

"Yes," she says.

Plates and bowls clink together. A fork clatters into the sink.

"She's in the kitchen," he says.

"Yes," she says. "She's stealing the silverware. It's lovely silverware. It belonged to my grandmother."

They hear the bathroom door open, then close.

"She's in the bathroom now," he says.

"Yes, she's stealing the towels. They're beautiful towels—imported from Italy. Handwoven in green and gold—did you know? I wonder if she'll leave me any."

He laughs softly.

She watches his face, his mouth breaking into a grin. Full lips and even teeth. She'll remember his touch: gentle like the rest of him. She wonders what she will tell him. "I feel controlled by you. When we walk down the street and you put your arm around me, your hand rests on my shoulder. Always." A subtle maneuver. As if he were guiding her. But where? A place where life stays its course, journeys no further. "Or when we stand to cross the street, to wait for a taxi, your eyes appraise me. Or when you say 'I love you,' knowing I don't want to hear. You are claiming me." It's my weakness, she thinks, that I give into his loving.

He watches her face, a gaze that brushes him lightly. Slightly critical. He tries to find in her eyes the date of her departure. If it's soon, he'll get over it, but later—two months, another season, a year—it will have been too long by then. And he won't find her in someone else, though he will look. He'll try. But he can't read her eyes.

"She's gone into the living room," he says.

"Yes, she's stealing the oak furniture. She'll have a little trouble getting it all out the door. I wonder if she'll ask us to help her. But maybe the neighbors will interfere . . ."

She's receded. He feels it suddenly. Soon (an-

other week? a few days? tomorrow possibly)
she'll have disappeared.

She lies facing him, thinking, I've ruptured his
sense of self, his privacy. I've brought him out of
the shadows and made him love me. He won't
want to go back. But knows I'll leave him.
Yesterday he asked me for a photo. Why do you
need a photo when you have me? But knows he
doesn't. Tomorrow I'll tell him. In the café.
Where he comes early to wait for me. And I arrive, coming up behind him. I see the nape of his
neck, slightly bent forward. He has a book and a
cup of coffee. He is a man, waiting. He looks up
from his book and sees me. Our eyes meet. He
smiles. I kiss him on the mouth.

He lies facing her, imprinting her on his mind.
He feels he's never really known a woman.
Never really loved. And now when it fills him,
and he wants to engulf himself and her in it, she
won't accept it. He will have this love, and it will
be stunted within him. Nothing to help it out of
him.

The front door opens and is locked from the
outside.

"She's leaving," he says.

"Yes, she took the silverware, the Italian towels, the oak furniture. Everything's gone now . . .
The apartment's bare."

He will have her image along with the sensation of loving her. He will have that too. His body
in the embrace of hers. That she has given him.

129

He will have that but he will also have the ache, a purplish bruise surrounding the wound.

She sees the clock. It's time for him to leave for work. And he will because he always does. He's responsible. Like his shoes. Sitting neatly, socks tucked inside, waiting while they make love.

He sees her look at the clock. It's time to be gone.

"When will I see you again?" he asks, as he always does, thinking each time she might answer differently, say, "No, not again . . ."

"Tomorrow," she says, "At five. In the café."

He presses her to him, his lips finding hers, "Tomorrow then."

Colophon

This book was designed by Allan Kornblum at Coffee House Press in Minneapolis, Minnesota. Hi Rez Studio in Grants Pass, Oregon provided output service for the Cochin text and Post Roman display. This book was printed on acid-free paper and was smyth sewn to ensure durability. The book was printed and bound by Edwards Brothers in Ann Arbor, Michigan.

The publisher thanks the following funders for assistance which helped make this book possible: the Bush Foundation; the Minnesota State Arts Board; the Jerome Foundation; General Mills Foundation; the National Endowment for the Arts, a federal agency; and major grants from the Andrew W. Mellon Foundation, and the Lila Wallace Reader's Digest Fund.

JUDITH PETROVICH

Jessica Treat was born in New Brunswick, Canada, raised in New England, and lived for a number of years in Mexico City. Her stories, prose poems, essays, and translations have appeared in numerous journals and anthologies, including *Ms.*, *Black Warrior Review*, *Epoch*, *American Literary Review*, *Quarterly West*, *3rd Bed*, and *Double Room*. Her second book, *Not a Chance*, stories and a novella, was published by Fiction Collective Two in 2000. The recipient of a Connecticut Commission on the Arts Award in Fiction, Treat is Associate Professor of English at Northwestern Connecticut Community College and lives with her son in northwestern Connecticut.